W9-AJT-707

AN AVALON ROMANCE

ACCIDENT-PRONE
Sheila Claydon

The end of a long-term relationship leaves interior designer Alex Moyer emotionally bruised. Determined to concentrate on her career, she is thrilled when her boss asks her to redesign a hotel in the Canary Islands.

Matt Anderson, the hotel's handsome owner, has emotional problems of his own, so when Alex starts to melt the ice around his heart, he tries to ignore it.

Alex proves hard to ignore, however, when Matt has to constantly rescue the accident-prone designer. After he steps in to save her from the clutches of the untrustworthy Francesco Pascual, things begin to get out of hand. It becomes clear that dating Alex was part of Francesco's bigger plan to cause the hotel to fail. On top of that, Matt and Alex are falling for each other, which doesn't suit either of them.

Can they ignore their growing mutual attraction as they attempt to foil Francesco? If they succeed, well, Alex will have to return to London anyway . . . won't she?

ACCIDENT-PRONE

•

Sheila Claydon

AVALON BOOKS
NEW YORK

Published by Avalon Books,
an imprint of Thomas Bouregy & Co., Inc.
New York, NY

Library of Congress Cataloging-in-Publication Data

Claydon, Sheila.
    Accident-prone / Sheila Claydon.
        p. cm.
    ISBN 978-0-8034-7615-8 (hardcover : acid-free paper)
    I. Title.
    PS3603.L395A27 2011
    813'.6—dc23
                                            2011025769

PRINTED IN THE UNITED STATES OF AMERICA
ON ACID-FREE PAPER
BY RR DONNELLEY, HARRISONBURG, VIRGINIA

For Richard with love

Chapter One

For one gut-wrenching moment Matt thought that the woman walking toward him was Adriana. Same dark curls and olive skin, same compact figure, same ridiculously high heels tapping across the airport concourse. He closed his eyes. When he opened them again, she was standing beside him while she anxiously scanned the crowd gathered around the arrivals gate.

He scowled. He really must get a grip. Close up she was nothing like Adriana. The curls were softer and shot with chestnut streaks, and her skin was honey-colored with a tiny smattering of freckles across her nose. What was the matter with him that he thought every small, dark-haired woman was his wife? Why, this one wasn't even dressed like Adriana. Instead of high gloss and sparkle, she was wearing varying shades of beige. The slouchy trousers and T-shirt, as well as the thin sweater tied around her shoulders, were obviously aimed at travel comfort rather than elegance. Only the shoes, copper-colored sandals with a four-inch heel, were a fashion statement, or perhaps they were just a protest at her lack of inches.

As if aware of his scrutiny, she turned her head and met his gaze. Widely spaced green eyes and a distinctly snub nose banished any last resemblance to Adriana. Then she smiled, and without warning, an emotion deep inside him that had been dormant for longer than he cared to remember woke with a jerk and unexpectedly launched into a series of back-flips.

Feeling as if all the air had been sucked out of him, he dragged in a deep breath and started to turn away. The woman

1

put a hand on his arm to stop him. Her voice, when she spoke, was low and slightly husky.

"I think you're waiting for me." She nodded toward the handwritten sign he was holding up so that the new contract designer who was flying in from the UK could make himself known. Miguel & Anderson, the name of Matt's company, was printed in thick black lettering, and because he was over six feet tall, he was able to wave it high above the throng of passengers milling about the arrivals hall.

Far too aware of the cool touch of her fingers on his over-heated arm, he backed away slightly as he shook his head. "I'm afraid not. I'm waiting for a Mr. Alex Moyer from Curzon Design."

Her smile widened to a wry grin as she held out her hand. "Alexandra Moyer. Alex! It's not the first time this has happened. I do apologize."

Matt gave an inward groan as he clasped her hand, which was small and surprisingly firm. If he had known that Alex Moyer was female, and especially this brand of pocket-sized, alarmingly attractive female, he would never have asked his friend Tom Curzon to supply a contract designer to help plan his hotel development.

"Matthew Anderson." He introduced himself with a curt nod. Then, dropping her hand as if it were on fire, he seized her suitcase and travel bag and began to push his way through the crowd toward the wide glass doors leading to the car park.

Alex had no option but to follow him, almost running in an attempt to keep up with his long strides, her large leather shoulder bag banging uncomfortably against her side. Finally, with an unladylike expletive, she gave up and let him go ahead. After a predawn start, a delay, and then a four-hour flight sitting next to a small child with a high-voltage voice and a runny nose, she wasn't in the sort of mood to take any flak. What was with this guy anyway? No greeting, no polite inquiry about her flight, not even a welcoming smile despite the fact that they were going to spend the next six months working together.

Irritated, she watched him stride ahead on long, denim-clad legs, his muscular arms flexed against the weight of her bags. A skinny white T-shirt, which revealed the lean contours of his back, was in dazzling contrast to the dark tan of his neck. She supposed he was a bit of a hunk if you liked your men mean and moody, but she decidedly did not.

"Manners maketh man," she muttered under her breath as she made her way to where he was stowing her luggage into the trunk of a dark blue SUV. Then her naturally sunny nature got the better of her, and she began to make excuses for him. Perhaps he was hot. After all, her flight had been delayed, so he had had a long wait. Or maybe he had an appointment to keep. There were a hundred and one things a busy property developer might have to do, each one more important than hanging around an airport waiting for a man who turned out to be a woman!

That's it, she decided. *He's embarrassed because he got it wrong. He thought he was meeting a man.* It was something she was used to, the downside of shortening her name to Alex. It was no big deal, and she would tell him so, put him at his ease and make a joke of it.

By the time she reached the car, he had slammed the trunk shut and was standing waiting for her, holding the passenger door open. Noticing that irritation seemed to be the uppermost expression on his face, she decided that now was probably not the time to discuss the mix-up over her name. Instead she gave him a smile of thanks and hauled herself up into the high seat using the doorway as leverage. She suddenly felt inordinately pleased that she had had the foresight to wear high heels instead of the more comfortable moccasins she usually traveled in. At least they gave her the extra inches she needed to avoid humiliation. Having to be helped up into a big brute of a car by someone whose whole body language said that he didn't want her around was not something she would have relished.

Independent to a fault but only five feet and one inch tall, she found herself spending far too much of her life developing strategies to reach things, and far too much of her money buying killer heels.

Matt walked around to the driver's door, an inscrutable expression hiding the panic that was building inside him as the dual images of her high-octane smile and the curvy outline of her figure, revealed as she climbed up into the SUV, burned themselves onto his brain. This was not going to happen! Not a second time, and especially not now when so much depended on developing the hotel in time for the Christmas season. He had to find a way of coping with this.

He drew deep, calming breaths as he slid into the driver's seat and gunned the ignition. Then he forced himself to speak and was surprised that his voice sounded so normal when his heart was pumping as if he had just finished a marathon.

"Sorry about rushing you like this, but we have a business appointment at four o'clock. I hope you don't mind being thrown in at the deep end, but it was the only day I could get this particular meeting arranged over the next couple of weeks."

He stared straight ahead as he spoke, concentrating on the traffic as he negotiated his way out of the airport and onto the road traveling north.

Alex experienced a stab of dismay. So soon! She had hoped for time to unpack and unwind after what had been a hectic fortnight of arrangements and project handovers so that she could take a six-month assignment in Tenerife without her absence affecting her UK clients.

As one of Curzon Design's more junior designers, she had been thrilled when Tom Curzon had called her into his office and offered her a contract in the Canary Islands, one that most of her colleagues would have killed for.

"I'm not being entirely altruistic," he had told her when he saw the delight on her face. "You're one of our most promising designers, Alex. And because Matt Anderson is looking for new ideas, I think you're just what he needs. You've a way of thinking outside the box that is refreshing and sometimes inspirational."

He had paused, allowing her time to absorb his rare compliment, then continued in a softer tone. "I also think that you could do with time away from England, a complete change of scene. The past year has been hard for you, and it shows."

Her eyes had clouded over as she acknowledged his words with a rueful sigh. Tom was referring to her split from Rory, her partner of three years. Sensationally handsome, outwardly charming, and charismatic, he was everything she was not. She had lived in his reflected glory, eagerly anticipating the time when they would get married and settle down with a family far away from the superficiality of their high-maintenance city life. Unfortunately she had forgotten to check her ambitions with Rory himself, who, when she unburdened herself to him after a particularly tiresome weekend of late-night partying, was horrified.

Within weeks he had moved out, leaving her with a hole where her heart used to be and a rental that took all her spare cash. His only explanation had been that he wasn't ready to be tied down. He had too much living to do, too many places to see.

Alex had watched him go with mixed feelings. Her sadness over the ending of what she had thought was a special relationship was tempered by an unexpected feeling of relief that she could now live a quieter life after years of deferring to Rory's almost manic need for social activity. Mostly, however, she had felt toe-curling embarrassment that she had gotten it so wrong. Totally humiliated, she had had to accept that he had never really loved her, and to live with the knowledge that all their friends would think she had driven him away with her neediness.

Not that she needed to have worried about their friends, because after the split, most of them had followed Rory's star, preferring his big spending and his sudden decisions to take off for a weekend's skiing or a trip to the coast to her more mundane need for security and love. Only Bethany, who was a friend from college, and Tom Curzon's wife, Elspeth, had been there to prop her up. Not that she had allowed them to do much propping. Determined to resurrect the independent spirit that Rory had almost extinguished with his continual demands on her time, she had deflected their sympathy with self-deprecating humor and immersed herself in work. Of course she had lost weight as well and for a while had developed shadows under her eyes from too much crying, but her career had blossomed as she completed one design project after another by working evenings and weekends. Her frenetic work pace allowed no time for introspection, no opportunity for regret. It became her life, replacing the dreams she had once had of a loving husband, a family, and a house in the country.

Then, after months of rattling around in what estate agents classified as a desirable residence—a glass and stainless steel apartment that was too big for two, let alone one—she had decided it was time to move on and found herself a small garden apartment near the river. The day she moved in, Bethany and Elspeth had arrived laden with Champagne and food from the local delicatessen and insisted on a spontaneous housewarming. Sitting at a battered wooden table on her minuscule lawn, they had raised their glasses to the future.

"You were too good for him, Alex." Bethany, never one to mince her words, repeated what she had been telling Alex on a regular basis ever since she had moved in with Rory. "He's the frog you never should have kissed!"

They had giggled then, buoyed up by Champagne and the warmth of a late-afternoon sun. Later, however, while washing the dishes after her guests had gone, Alex had considered Bethany's words anew. What had gone wrong between her and Rory? Had their relationship broken down because she had expected too much from him, or had she just been so spellbound by his good looks and charisma that she had let him selfishly override her own needs until it was almost too late?

What had he wanted from her anyway? She had no illusions about herself. She knew she was attractive, but she wasn't stunning, not in the way that many of Rory's friends' girlfriends were. She knew that she had style, but she was too impatient to spend her time on facials and manicures, or spend hours straightening her thick, curly hair, so her finish was never quite as high gloss or contrived. She knew, too, that she could be good company, just not in a way that made her central to any social gathering, because she was a listener rather than a talker, content to sit on the sidelines while Rory held court.

Was that why he had been attracted to her? Had she just been someone who wouldn't outshine him, someone who would gaze adoringly at him and not compete? She felt something inside her shrivel as her self-confidence took a nosedive. How could she have been so stupid? How could she have been so craven? There and then she made up her mind never to open up her heart so trustingly again. Bethany had been right. Rory was a frog, and if she met another one, she would throw him right back into the pond.

That had been almost eighteen months ago, and now, after a long, wet winter that had seen her trudging from project to project around a dismal city whose roads were in almost perpetual gridlock, she was looking forward to six months of sun, with sea and sand thrown in for good measure.

She glanced across at Matt. He was still looking straight ahead, and he didn't appear to care whether she concurred with his meeting arrangements or not. For a moment her irritation returned; then she shrugged. *What the heck!* As long as she could shake her brain cells into shape after such an early start, she might as well get on with the job. It was going to be a challenge anyway. She had already seen pictures and plans of the hotel Miguel & Anderson were hoping to refit in time for the Christmas season, and she knew it was going to be a push to finish the project on time.

"I guess I can manage a meeting if you brief me," she said. "But I would like to freshen up if possible. It's been a long day so far."

For the first time he glanced across at her and, easier in her presence now that they were talking work, suddenly noticed her tangled hair and drawn expression. He shook his head in something close to self-disgust.

"I'm sorry. I should have realized you'd be tired. This hotel project has taken over my life to the extent that I tend to forget about the niceties. Rufino says that if he and Cristina didn't feed me occasionally, I'd starve to death."

"Rufino Miguel, your business partner?"

"Yes. You're staying with him and his wife Cristina tonight," he continued. "Cristina insisted. She said you'd need some care and attention after your journey, so I'm sure she's cooking up a storm. She's going to help you move into your apartment tomorrow too."

Alex immediately warmed to the unknown Cristina. It had been a long time since she had stayed with anyone other than her parents, and now that they were retired and spent half their lives taking last-minute holidays, her visits home were few and far between. This was something that had started when she was with Rory and she had noticed how bored he was by their travel tales, and she felt ashamed that she had never quite put it right since. She pushed away unwelcome thoughts with an exclamation of pleasure.

"How kind of her! I thought I'd be staying in a hotel to start with."

"And enjoying the pleasures of solitary eating." He shook his head, the ghost of a smile hovering around his lips as he pulled out to overtake a truck. "You'll soon learn that that's not the Canarian way. In fact, once Cristina realizes my mistake, you'll probably have to fight her and her friends off in order to find enough time to do your work!"

For a moment Alex was puzzled; then she realized that he was referring to the fact that, because of the mix-up over her name, he, and consequently Rufino and Cristina, had all been expecting a male colleague. Deciding that now was the time to put him at ease about it, she launched into a series of amusing anecdotes of similar situations, before finally admitting that maybe she should tell Tom to be more specific in future. Although he made no comment, he smiled once or twice and even glanced across at her again. Relieved that he was finally showing signs of thawing, she decided that, having done her party piece for the good of their future working relationship, she could now sit back and enjoy the view.

Because she had never visited the Canary Islands, she had looked up Tenerife on the Internet so she wouldn't be completely at a loss in business meetings. A speed read through several links had shown her that it was one of a chain of volcanic islands in the Atlantic Ocean off the coast of Africa. She had also learned that because of its year-round sunshine it was a major tourist destination for vacationers from the UK as well as from other countries in northern Europe. Apart from that she knew very little, and even less about the town where Miguel & Anderson had its office, so she watched the passing scenery with interest and with something akin to excited anticipation, a feeling she hadn't had in a long, long time.

Although air-conditioning kept the car comfortably cool and a tinted windshield protected them from the glare of the sun, she knew from her short walk across the airport parking lot that outside the heat was considerable. It was a dry heat lifted by a slight breeze, the sort of heat that invaded muscles and bones and soothed the aches and pains of a long, cold winter as readily as it lifted the spirits and was balm to the soul.

With a skin that tanned easily, as well as a love of the outdoors, Alex could hardly wait to shed the grayness of winter. After months of solitary grieving for what might have been, she was now in recovery and was going to wrest as much enjoyment as possible from her enforced trip, although she had no intention of shortchanging Miguel & Anderson while she did so. Used to long hours and determined to stay footloose and fancy-free, she couldn't think of a single thing that would interfere with her plan.

As Matt drove along the coast, fields of protective polytunnels were replaced by small banana plantations, giant palms, and impossibly twisted cacti, all interspersed with brightly colored flowers set among rocky outcrops. Steep hills climbed away from the road, while on the coastal side the sea shone like shot silk in the afternoon sun.

Soon they were passing through small towns full of apartments, their balconies fluttering with bright canvas canopies and an occasional line of washing. Then it was high-rise hotels, where tourist coaches were delivering batches of vacationers fresh from the airport. Caught up in the kaleidoscope of color as the car sped westward, she forgot about Matt, so when he spoke, she jumped.

"It's only a few miles now. We'll be in the office by three thirty, which will give you time to freshen up and have some coffee. I use a couple of rooms at the top of the building to crash when I'm working late. It's pretty basic, I'm afraid, but I can dig up a clean towel, and the water is hot."

Chapter Two

Crash pad just about described it, Alex decided fifteen minutes later as she followed him up two steep flights of stairs to a cramped attic accommodation at the top of a square, white-painted building on the outskirts of the town.

The offices of Miguel & Anderson occupied the first two floors. Although not at all grand, they were cool and professional. Marble tiling in shades of cream was complemented by dark wood and modern desks. The four computers, each with a webcam, were recent models, all of which Alex found encouraging.

A pretty, dark-haired woman in her midtwenties had greeted them when they arrived. She had tried not to stare at Alex as she relayed a series of messages to Matt in Spanish. He listened intently and then, with his cell phone already clamped to one ear, had made hasty introductions in English.

"Conchita, this is Alexandra Moyer, our new designer. Alex, this is Conchita Eberardo, Miguel & Anderson's office manager. Without her, we couldn't function! She's related to half the people living on Tenerife, so we get to hear about new properties coming onto the market before the owner has decided to sell. On top of that, because she is power mad, she insists on maintaining a filing system that's a complete mystery to the rest of us, so we're entirely at her mercy, right down to where she keeps the coffee filters."

Startled by the warmth in his voice after her own cool reception, Alex was surprised into looking at him properly for the first time.

Blue eyes, she noticed. Really bright blue, under straight brows and framed by thick brown lashes. And his teeth were the sort of very square white teeth that make a smile doubly attractive, particularly when it's set off by curved lips and the shadow of a dimple in one cheek. His hair, which she decided was in need of a cut, was thick and wavy and streaked dirty blond by the sun.

As if he was aware that she was staring at him, he had stopped teasing Conchita and glanced across at Alex just as the person he was calling answered the phone. For one long moment their eyes had met and held. Then he had turned away and concentrated on his phone call. For some unaccountable reason, Alex had felt a tide of warmth wash through her, flushing her cheeks and leaving her breathless. Conchita, however, had given her no time to collect her scattered thoughts.

"Alex Moyer . . . so you are not a man! Fantastic!" She had dismissed Matt's joking introduction with a flip of her hand. "Take no notice of him. He talks rubbish! I need a girl around here for some solidarity!"

Alex had laughed and held out her hand. "I like your style, Conchita. Never let them get to you. Life's too short!"

For a second time her eyes had met Matt's, but this time he was frowning, all the warmth he had directed at Conchita replaced by a cool disregard. Alex wasn't sure if he had heard her flippant remark and disapproved, or if he was just responding to something that was being said to him on the telephone. Whatever it was, she had decided that she would ignore him. Moodiness was an unpleasant trait, and if it was part of Matthew Anderson's character, then it was one she didn't intend to lose any sleep over. She was here to work, not to be best friends with the boss.

Now, as she reached the tiny landing at the top of the stairs, she almost collided with him as he stopped to open a door. Indicating that she should follow him into the small sitting-room-cum-kitchen that took up half of the top floor of the building, he began to rummage in a cupboard for a towel.

Finding one, he held it out to her and then pushed open the door to what was obviously his bedroom. Explaining that the bathroom was en suite, he backed out of the room.

"I'll be downstairs when you're ready. And Conchita is brewing some coffee."

"Thank you." Alex clutched the towel to her chest, hoping that her embarrassment didn't show. She had no idea why she felt uncomfortable. Obviously Matt was perfectly relaxed about her invasion of his private crash pad, and it was remarkably tidy. The bed was made and draped with a dark blue blanket. Blue-and-white checkered curtains were blowing in the breeze of an open window, and there was a striped cotton rug on the tiled floor. Apart from that and a built-in wardrobe, the room was empty and impersonal. There were no photographs, no pictures, not even a hairbrush or a bottle of men's cologne on the windowsill.

"Take your time," he added as he retreated down the stairs. "I can hold the meeting for an extra ten minutes or so."

Left to her own devices, Alex pushed open the door to the tiny bathroom in trepidation. All her bathroom dealings with Rory had involved dropped clothes and the clutter of hair gel, tubes of topless toothpaste, discarded dental floss, pre-shave, aftershave, and a hundred and one other things. He was always buying new "must-have" toiletries while rarely discarding old ones, until his growing regimen of bottles had eventually jostled her own small supply off the shelf and onto a corner of the windowsill.

Matt's bathroom, however, was as pristine as his bedroom. Anything he used was hidden in the bathroom cabinet, except for a solitary toothbrush in a blue plastic mug and some shower gel in the shower.

Not a love nest then, she told herself, acknowledging that for some reason her embarrassment had all to do with intruding on his personal life. Slightly bothered by such uncharacteristic squeamishness on her part, she tried to dismiss him from her mind as she dropped the towel onto a low wooden stool and turned on the tap. As he had promised, the water was plentiful and hot, and ten minutes later, feeling refreshed and clean, she cast a last look at herself in the square mirror over the basin before descending the stairs to the office. When she arrived, Conchita greeted her with a smile, a full mug of rich, dark coffee, and a plate of bite-sized cakes.

"You look better now," she approved, taking in the fresh makeup and the gloss of newly brushed hair. "Less travel-weary."

"Thanks, Conchita." Alex was grateful for her approval. "I hope I look okay for the meeting Matt has arranged. After all, first impressions count."

"You'll be fine." Conchita dismissed her fears with a puff of the lips. "It will do all those men good to have to listen to a pretty girl for a change, especially one who knows what she's talking about."

Not entirely sure that she did know what she was meant to be talking about, because Matt had not gotten around to briefing her on their more or less silent journey from the airport, Alex followed the other woman into what was obviously his office.

Immediately the drone of conversation halted and four men rose to their feet, including Matt. He introduced her, passed her a copy of the plans they were studying, and then brought her up to speed.

For the next hour she listened as they discussed technical details and their concern that nothing should delay the completion. The meeting was conducted in English for her benefit, but occasionally one of the men was forced to resort to Spanish when a word proved elusive. Each time this happened he bowed and apologized.

"Please don't worry," she begged at last. "I'm only sorry that my Spanish isn't good enough to make things easier for you."

"You speak Spanish?" Matt looked surprised. "Tom didn't say."

"That's because it's only schoolgirl Spanish," she explained. "I can get by in a restaurant or ask the way if I'm lost, but I don't know any of the technical stuff, so I'm afraid it's not much use at all as far as work is concerned."

"It's still better than nothing." He gave her a look that might have been approval. "In this job you have to talk to all sorts of people, so even a smattering of Spanish might prove useful at times, especially when you answer the telephone."

Knowing her limitations, Alex immediately decided to stay as far away from the office telephone as possible. Nevertheless she found Matt's words and the look of approbation that he had given her replaying themselves in her head. She forced herself to concentrate on the discussion continuing around the table. How ridiculous to react like that just because he approved of something as simple as her tenuous grasp of the local language. She must be more tired than she realized.

The meeting over, everyone shook hands, and soon only Alex and Matt were left in the office, Conchita having shut down her computer and gone home while they were still in conference.

"You did well," he said. "You grasped everything really quickly—quite a feat in a foreign country, and after the journey you've had."

"Thanks." She stowed the papers from the meeting in her bag so that she could read them again later. "I'm used to thinking on my feet because Tom runs a tight schedule. His motto is 'Time is money!' "

"Still the same old Tom, then." Matt gave a chuckle of recognition. It was the first time she had seen him relax, and much to her consternation, the glint of laughter in those blue, blue eyes unexpectedly inserted a sliver of warmth into the place where her heart used to be, a place that she thought she had closed down forever.

Chapter Three

Much later, replete after a meal of fish served with a green salsa, tiny baked potatoes, and a tomato salad, Alex sipped the last of her wine and listened to Rufino and Cristina reminiscing about a touring holiday they had once had in England.

"We ended up in the Yorkshire Dales," remembered Rufino.

Cristina nodded. "Yes, and the scenery was beautiful—all soft curves lit by pale sunshine and shadow—and so many sheep! Even the food was good most of the time," she added in her attractively accented English. "It wasn't at all what we expected. We had heard so many bad things about England and its weather."

"You were just lucky." Matt held his empty wineglass out for a refill. "Usually it's gray and wet, or cold and wet, or windy and wet, or just wet. Why do you think I've settled over here? What's to choose between wet and continuous sunshine?"

"That is such an exaggeration!" Alex protested as Rufino topped up her glass. "We have loads of good weather. Think of all the poets who've written about the wonders of the English spring."

"That's just because after so many months of rain, it always comes as a surprise to them," he countered, with the ghost of a teasing smile.

"Stop it, Matt!" Cristina reached out and slapped his hand as if he were a recalcitrant child. "It's bad enough that you first thought that Alex was going to be a man, and then you made her attend a meeting the moment she arrived without even offering her lunch. Now you insult her beautiful country

16

too. Whatever will she think of you, of all of us, after such a welcome?"

"You've more than compensated for all my deficiencies." Matt gave her an affectionate look as he drained his glass and pushed back his chair. "As always, that was a wonderful meal, Cristina. Rufino is a lucky man! Now I must go."

"Not before you have truly welcomed Alex to Tenerife," insisted Cristina as Rufino busied himself with a bottle of dark liqueur and four small glasses.

"An island tradition at the end of a meal," he told Alex as he handed her a full glass. "Welcome to Tenerife, island of sunshine. May your stay be a truly happy one."

The others raised their glasses.

"*Salud.*" Matt downed the contents of his in one swallow and then stood up, lazily uncoiling his long, lean body from the seat opposite Alex.

Dear God, there it goes again. He groaned inwardly as their eyes met and held. All through the evening he had been tormented by her closeness. Her every movement and every word had been a signal for his treacherous body to launch into the wild somersault routine that had started at the airport. He had forced himself to act normally. To make conversation. To pick up his knife and fork. To eat. He knew that he looked relaxed. Knew that none of the others had a clue about what he was going through. It was a skill that he had perfected long ago to deflect the highly charged emotional scenes that had been so much a part of his marriage to Adriana, but he wasn't sure if he could keep it up for much longer. He needed time away from Alex. Time to free his senses from the intoxicating scent of her. Time to marshal his wayward thoughts into some sort of order. He also needed a very cold shower!

"I'll leave my car here if that's okay," he said. "I've drunk far too much wine to drive home."

"Shall I call a taxi?" Cristina was already dialing when he shook his head.

"No thanks. The jog will do me good. I've been sitting down all day."

She raised her eyes heavenward. "You are always exercising! What's wrong with sitting down for a day?"

He leaned down and dropped a kiss onto the top of her head. "Nothing, if you like grumpy! Jogging keeps me sweet. Thanks again for a lovely meal."

"Go!" She pushed him toward the door. "Go! Go! Go! I will bring Alex to the office tomorrow after I have helped her settle into her apartment."

He paused on his way out the door and steeled himself to look across at Alex again. "Why don't you take the whole day?" he suggested casually. "That way you'll get Cristina off my back for working you too hard as soon as you arrive, plus it will give you time to get settled."

"Thanks." Alex gave him that huge, warm smile again, the one that set his heart pumping double time. "I would really appreciate that. I promise I'll be bright-eyed and bushy-tailed on Wednesday morning."

He waved his approval and turned away, calling out his good-byes as he took to the road. At least he had given himself twenty-four hours respite, twenty-four hours to tame his body and force his heart back into the dark, still place inside him where it belonged.

It took him half an hour to cover the distance back to his solitary bed above the office, and with each step he took, every detail of Alex's face became more deeply imprinted upon his brain.

Alex started to clear the table as Matt headed out the door. Cristina gave a cry of protest when she saw her and seized the pile of plates that she was holding.

"Enough! You are our guest, and a very tired one too! Off you go to bed. I've put lavender in your pillow to help you sleep well."

Alex accepted her offer with a grateful smile. She was indeed tired, and although she had only met Cristina a few hours previously, she already knew that arguing was pointless. Plump and pretty in a red dress and with a cloud of black curls caught up in a vivid scarf, Cristina was one of life's nurturers, only truly happy when she was in charge of a full table and a full house.

When Alex and Matt had eventually arrived for supper that evening—later than expected because Matt had had to make some telephone calls, and Alex had been keen to familiarize herself with her desk and the office in general—Cristina had scolded them for being so late while lavishing hugs and kisses in equal measure. Then she had inspected Alex at arm's length and pronounced her tired and too thin.

Given her city winter pallor and the fact that her clothes no long clung to her, Alex didn't feel that this took great powers of deduction. She did not, however, take exception to such a personal opinion because Cristina's welcome was warm and her smile of approval, as she openly admired Alex's long, shiny curls, perfect skin, and stylish clothes, was balm to her soul.

Since Rory's defection she had felt mediocre, the sort of person who would go unnoticed in a crowd. Always larger than life, Rory had been impossible to ignore, and until he left her, Alex hadn't realized how much her confidence had depended on his social ease and his charismatic good looks. Once he was no longer there to prop her up, she felt very ordinary. As his partner she had always been able to pretend that she, too, was scintillating company, that the never-ending invitations littering the notice board in the kitchen were personal. Only when it all fell apart did she realize how much she had deluded herself and accept that she would never stand out in any social situation, because there would always be other women who were more beautiful, more intelligent, more confident, and more together. If she was totally honest, it didn't bother her most of the time, but just occasionally she missed the approbation. Even the insincere flattery of Rory's friends had had the effect of boosting her confidence, so when she saw the genuine admiration in Cristina's dark brown eyes, a part of her that had been starved for too long began to bloom.

Rufino, too, had smiled at her so approvingly and bent over her hand so gallantly, that she had half believed him when he said that they were truly honored to have her as a guest, and she had chosen to ignore the little voice in her head that told her that he probably greeted everyone that way.

It was such a happy house that even Matt had relaxed as he stepped over the threshold, his serious expression giving way to something softer and more approachable. It was obvious, too, from his smiling reaction to Cristina's scolding and Rufino's amicable teasing, that they were old and treasured friends.

Now, alone in the guest bedroom at the top of the house, Alex pondered the evening as she got ready for bed. She didn't know if it was the generous flow of wine or the warmth of her welcome, but whatever it was, she had had a nice time. In fact, a nicer time than she had had in a long while.

Wine, accompanied by a selection of tapas, had been followed by a proud tour of the house. Leaving the men to barbecue the prepared fish, Cristina had insisted on showing her every nook and cranny of her recently refurbished home, explaining that after months of waiting she had eventually shamed Rufino into completing the work he had promised when they moved in.

"There's a Spanish saying, '*En casa de herrero, cuchillo de pal*,' which means the shoemaker's son always goes barefoot," she explained. "But in the end I became so fed up with waiting and waiting while Rufino and Matt started yet another project, pushing me again to the back of the pile, that I had a tantrum!"

"We have similar sayings in England." Alex laughed, quite sure that Cristina's tantrum would have been something so spectacular that her husband would have had no choice but to comply with her demands.

They had ended the tour by tiptoeing into the nursery where Cristina and Rufino's two-year-old twin boys were fast asleep, each with flushed cheeks under a tousle of black curls, their arms thrown wide and their legs akimbo.

"Don't be lulled into thinking they're angels just because they're the picture of innocence," whispered Rufino, who had come to tell them that the fish was ready. "They're monsters, the pair of them. Only fit company when they're asleep."

Their mother laughed as she spread thin blankets over them. "Take no notice. He adores them!"

"They're absolutely gorgeous." Alex took a final look at the two little boys, who were fast asleep among a pile of soft toys, and felt her heart contract. This was what she had wanted, what she had thought Rory had wanted too. But when she saw the look of love mingled with pride that Rufino gave his wife and his children as he left the room, she suddenly realized how wrong Rory would have been. In fact, now that time had distanced the hurt and rejection, she could only wonder at her naïveté. How had she ever thought for a moment that someone as selfish and self-centered as Rory would be able to contemplate the inevitable boundaries of family life?

Returning to the dining area, to where wide glass doors opened onto a terrace that looked across a bay streaked red and gold from the setting sun, they found Matt adding some oil and garnish to the succulent fish. The appetizing aroma of barbecue made Alex realize how hungry she was. She had only managed a few olives and two cubes of cheese from the tapas before Cristina had invited her to inspect the house. Now, sitting in the fading light while Rufino lit strategically placed lanterns, she had to grab at her manners to stop herself from picking up her knife and fork before he joined them at the table. Everything looked and smelled so delicious that her mouth was actually watering!

Conversation during the rest of the evening was as varied as it was interesting. Alex learned that Cristina and Rufino had met when she joined Miguel & Anderson as an administrator, and that she still did their accounts.

"It was love over a paper clip," Matt quipped.

"I so enjoyed working," Cristina sighed, "but then I was pregnant, and two small babies and work don't mix."

"Heaven forbid!" exclaimed Rufino in horror. "The thought of those two let loose in the office doesn't bear thinking about! Conchita would have a fit."

"Conchita is their godmother. She loves them." Cristina aimed for dignity but ended up squealing with mirth at the thought of her children invading the pristine confines of Miguel & Anderson.

Amid the general laughter, however, it quickly became clear that she still had her finger on the pulse. As well as knowing everything about Alex's contract, she had decided views about the proposed plan to renovate the Alcaszar, a run-down hotel that had once seen better times, and which was Alex's design project.

"It could be wonderful," she declared. "It just needs some imagination."

"Well, that's what Alex is here for," said Matt.

After that they spent the rest of the evening discussing the hotel and how they hoped to restore it to its former glory in order to attract a different sort of tourist to the town.

"This is an area of carefully planned low-rise apartments with only a couple of multistory hotels," explained Matt, animated now that he was talking about work. "It's the sort of place people return to again and again because it's small and tranquil and has an air of exclusivity about it. The fact that it's closed in on all sides by cliffs and by the Atlantic Ocean makes it special. We also get a lot of private boats visiting the marina. What we don't have, however, is a really prestigious hotel, somewhere that provides a specialized service for the people with real money who want to get away from it all. The Alcaszar has that potential. It has the view and the history. We just need to make it happen."

Inspired by his enthusiasm, Alex could hardly wait to see the hotel. She already had some outline ideas but wanted to view the site before she shared them. She asked a lot of questions, however, and then watched, fascinated, as he used napkins and knives and forks to map different parts of the complex, his strong brown fingers deft, his blue eyes glowing as he described his dream.

Now, with her teeth cleaned and her hair brushed, she sat cross-legged in the middle of the bed and gazed thoughtfully out the window to where she could still see the flicker of distant lights across the bay. The night was so warm that even with the casement thrown wide, her strappy pajamas were sufficient.

She had had a wonderful evening full of warmth and welcome. So what was it that was bothering her? This was a dream job, exciting and challenging. The six months on Tenerife were a bonus that she was determined to fully enjoy. Cristina and Rufino were fantastic. Yet something was wrong. She thought about the evening again and suddenly realized what it was. Despite spending hours in his company, she still knew nothing whatsoever about Matthew Anderson.

Cristina and Rufino had not only talked about their own lives but had asked Alex about hers. She had told them that she had a much older brother who lived in New Zealand. She had also talked about her nieces and nephew and how much she had enjoyed her single trip to visit them all several years ago. Then they had asked about her parents and about her own life and so had learned that she liked to swim and walk, that she was an avid reader, a keen cook, and an amateur gardener. And because she didn't want to sound too boring, she had also regaled them with stories of her social life in London, omitting the fact that all of its more colorful aspects were now in the past.

Throughout it all Matt had sat and listened, occasionally meeting her eyes across the top of his wineglass but rarely commenting. Not once during the evening had he offered any information about his own life, and surprisingly, given their openness about themselves, neither had Cristina and Rufino.

He was still a complete mystery. He was serious. He seemed moody. Yet this evening had shown that there was a warmth to him too, a kindness that he camouflaged with jokes and teasing repartee. Always a people watcher, Alex was intrigued. She had been into his attic apartment above the office, had walked through his bedroom, used his bathroom, all without gaining any idea of who he was, what made him tick. His living accommodations were plain to the point of impersonal. He seemed to spend all his time working. In fact, he only really came alive when he talked about work. Why would a man as attractive as Matthew Anderson choose to live such a monastic life?

Yawning, she pulled back the white cotton covers of her bed and settled herself against the pillows. It was a mystery that would have to wait, because she could not stay awake a moment longer. She drifted into sleep soothed by the scent of lavender and the distant sound of waves crashing against the rocky shore, barely aware that eyes as blue as the Tenerife sky invaded her dreams.

Chapter Four

Waking early the following morning, Alex lay in bed and listened to the sounds of the house. She heard the murmur of Cristina's voice and then little fluting sounds like birdsong. It took her a moment to realize that it was the twins, who had woken and were calling. Soon the sounds grew louder, and then she heard the patter of small feet on the wooden floor. Slowly her door was pushed open, and two sets of sparkling black eyes peeped in at her.

"*Hola,*" she said, guessing that they probably understood only Spanish.

Immediately they disappeared to the sound of much giggling. Smiling, she swung her feet onto the floor and welcomed the new day with a luxurious stretch. She felt more rested and relaxed than she had in months, and she was looking forward to settling into her new home and starting work.

Twenty minutes later, showered and dressed in casual clothes, she gave her hair a final brush before descending into the kitchen. There, ensconced in matching high chairs and covered from chin to toes in plastic bibs, sat Luis and Nicolas. Cristina was standing between them with an air of despairing pride on her face as she fielded cups of milk, pieces of bread, and slices of banana.

"I never remember how awful it is," she groaned. "I suppose it must be self-protection to stop me from going entirely mad!"

Alex laughed as she removed a portion of well-chewed bread from the table and dropped it into the trash can.

"Can I help?" she asked.

"No! They will only ruin your clothes, to say nothing of your sanity." Cristina grinned at her. "Help yourself to coffee. Fruit and rolls are on the table."

Alex poured a cup of steaming coffee from the percolator and then pulled out a chair. The breakfast looked delicious. A selection of fruit was piled into a bowl next to a dish of creamy yogurt and a plate of rolls that were still warm from the oven. Choosing a ripe peach, she sliced it into a blue and yellow bowl and spooned yogurt over it.

After a few minutes Cristina joined her, having wiped the worst of the stickiness from her sons' hands and faces and furnished them with paper and crayons.

"That should keep them occupied for at least five minutes." She sighed. "And by then Mama will have arrived. She looks after them whenever I'm desperate, and today I'm desperate."

"They're beautiful children," Alex said. "You're so lucky to have them."

As she spoke, the door opened wide and a woman who was a shorter, stouter version of Cristina came into the kitchen laden with bags that she dumped on the floor. Luis and Nicolas yelled with excitement when they saw her and held up their arms. Addressing them in rapid Spanish, she smothered them in kisses as she released them from their wooden chairs. As soon as they were free, they wriggled out of her grasp and, making a beeline for the bags, began a systematic search that unearthed shiny toy trucks, two coloring books, and a packet of chocolate.

Cristina's remonstrations were met with another torrent of Spanish as her mother kissed her on both cheeks and then produced melons, salad greens, and tomatoes from the depths of another bag, all of them fresh from her garden. She added a large muslin-wrapped goat cheese to the pile and then waited to be introduced to Alex, her face wreathed in smiles.

"*Hola. Buenos días.*" Alex, hoping that her very rusty Spanish was sufficient, was rewarded by an even wider smile and a nod of approval.

For the next few minutes she managed a very basic conversation while Cristina tidied her hair and found her cell phone and keys. Then Alex ran back upstairs to collect her overnight bag and carried it out to Cristina's car.

After kissing Luis and Nicolas and calling out final instructions to her mother, Cristina slid into the driver's seat with a mischievous grin that was so reminiscent of that of her small sons that it made Alex laugh.

"A whole day to ourselves," Cristina said. "No sticky fingers, no constant demands, no need for four pairs of hands, just a civilized lunch and some gentle shopping. I'll show you your new home, and then we'll go to the market so that you can stock up your cupboards."

Ten minutes later Alex unlocked the door to the lemon-colored apartment that was to be her home for the next six months. Set at the end of a row, it nestled into the hillside, blue shutters tightly closed over small square windows. At the front door, pots of brightly colored geraniums jostled for position with other more exotic plants that she didn't recognize.

Inside, the whitewashed walls and high ceilings were relieved by soft drapes patterned in muted creams and blues. Simple pine furniture and squashy pale sofas piled high with orange and blue cushions gave an impression of light and space even before Cristina pulled back the heavy blinds that blocked out the sun and opened the doors to the balcony.

For a moment Alex was speechless. A tumble of orange and yellow bougainvillea covered the stone walls of the balcony, while tier upon tier of flat-roofed apartments climbed down the hillside below in blocks of pastel stone. Cream, pink, yellow, white, they were set against a backdrop of glittering sea and a pale blue sky. She turned to Cristina, who was leaning on the balustrade beside her.

"It's beautiful. I'd no idea that I was going to live in such an idyllic place. My colleagues in the UK will be so jealous when I tell them!"

Cristina smiled at her delight. "This was Matt's first home. Even then he knew how to pick the best spot. And now he owns the whole block."

"Does he live in one of the other apartments?" Alex grabbed at the first piece of information that she had been given about Matt.

"Gracious, no! He moved up into the mountains years ago. For someone who spends his life buying and developing holiday properties, he has a strong aversion to tourists and tourist entertainment. He prefers to live as far away from town as possible."

"I suppose that's why he keeps a crash pad over the office. He lives too far away to drive home when he's been working late." Alex was thinking aloud, not really expecting an answer to a conundrum that she had already solved to her own satisfaction, so she was surprised when Cristina shook her head.

"No, I don't think the drive bothers him. I think he just finds his house too full of the memories of his marriage. Rufino and I have noticed that he doesn't seem able to spend time alone there anymore, and we wonder why he doesn't sell it. Admittedly it's in a wonderful spot, with views to die for, but that's not everything. He needs to move on, to leave his sadness behind and make a fresh start somewhere else."

Alex stared at her and then looked back at the wonderful view, her green eyes clouded with pity. So that was the mystery of Matthew Anderson. Something very simple that would never have occurred to her. It explained his serious demeanor, his moodiness, and the brooding intensity in his eyes. He was a grieving widower.

"Has he been alone very long?" she asked, but Cristina had gone back into the apartment to inspect the rest of the rooms and didn't hear her.

Later, sitting with Cristina at a restaurant close to the marina and eating a simple goat cheese salad, Alex wondered whether to bring up the subject of Matt's status again. After all, she was going to be working closely with him, so the last thing she wanted to do was open old wounds by saying or doing the wrong thing. On the other hand, Cristina was his friend, so she might not appreciate a virtual stranger asking intimate questions about him or his dead wife. Before she could make up her mind, however, the waiter arrived with the bill, ending all possibility of further discussion, and soon they were wending their way back up the hill to the apartment.

"I guess I need to get fit," she puffed as the steep incline pulled at her calf muscles. "Is the entire island like this?"

Cristina laughed, striding up what seemed to be an almost vertical road without any difficulty. "There are lots of places with easier walking, but none of them are as pretty."

Alex paused for breath and looked about her. It was beautiful. The morning's exertions had introduced her to a small town of narrow pavements with flights of steps climbing down between the houses to hidden roads, and into squares full of canopied tables set for lunch with fresh white cloths and napkins, their cutlery and glasses gleaming in the sun. Shops lined the busier roads, small boutiques and jewelers cheek by jowl with mini-markets, fruit shops, and flower stalls. Farther up the hill, leading away from the center, was a cluster of offices, each hidden from public view by vertical blinds but with doors propped open to let in the soft breeze that wafted the sweet perfume of flowers across the streets. And there were flowers everywhere: swathes of purple jacaranda, spiky cacti growing in grotesque shapes or blooming with exotic orange flowers, hibiscus and bougainvillea in a multitude of colors, all growing against a backdrop of graceful palms.

Everything was so perfect that it seemed impossible that only yesterday she had left a rain-sodden London behind. Hurrying to catch up with Cristina, who was waiting patiently at the top of the hill, she failed to notice someone stepping out of an open doorway, his arms piled high with books, and they collided, causing her to lose her balance. Strong fingers gripped her upper arm, catching her before she fell.

"*Lo siento!*" a deep voice apologized. "*Ha sido sin querer.*"

"*No importa,*" she replied as she found herself looking up into a pair of laughing black eyes set beneath wavy dark hair. Then she looked down in consternation at the scatter of books across the pavement and reverted to English. "I'm so sorry! I wasn't looking where I was going. I was too busy admiring the view. Let me help you pick up your books."

"You must be new to the island." Her rescuer immediately switched to strongly accented English as they both bent to retrieve his belongings. "Locals never stop to look at the view—it's too familiar! Are you here on holiday?"

"No . . . I mean, yes." Alex became slightly confused as she noticed the boldness of his gaze. "That is, I'm new to the island, but I'm not on holiday. I'm here to work. For Miguel & Anderson Property Developers," she added as he raised an inquiring eyebrow.

"Then fortunately we will meet again, because Cristina Miguel is my cousin." He held out his hand. "Francesco Pascual."

"Alexandra Moyer . . . Alex." She tried to ignore the fact that he was holding her hand for a fraction too long. She tried, too, to ignore the way his Spanish accent imbued his words with a certain sexiness, and the way his black eyes openly admired her. After all, this was what she wanted, what she needed: an adventure, someone to share it with, some fun, and it looked as if she might have just met the one person who could supply all three.

She dimpled up at him through her eyelashes, deliberately flirting before she turned away. "I will look forward to that, Francesco."

And as she made her way toward Cristina, she knew that he was watching her and taking in the neat curve of her rear in her tight blue cutoffs and the elusive glimpse of bare skin beneath her short white T-shirt, and for the first time in a very long time she felt sexy and desirable. Shaking back her curls, she held her head high and her back straight and introduced just the tiniest hint of a wiggle into her walk.

Cristina waved to Francesco Pascual as she greeted Alex with a grin. "I see you don't waste much time. But neither does Francesco. He's the local heartthrob, and he knows it, but you could do worse. He'll give you a good time and show you Tenerife into the bargain."

And that, thought Alex, *is exactly what I'm looking for.*

Chapter Five

 Alex arrived at Miguel & Anderson's office at eight thirty the following morning after an evening spent settling into her new home. She had refused Cristina's offer of an evening meal but had agreed to meet up again later in the week.

After unpacking her clothes and putting the food she had bought at the market into the kitchen cupboards, she had made herself a coffee and taken it onto her balcony to enjoy the last of the evening sun. When it turned into a spectacular sunset that bathed the roofs below her in pink and gold, she congratulated herself anew on her good fortune and decided that she would make the most of this unexpected chance to stay in such a beautiful, sunny place. She would use it to provide the energy she needed to restart her social life. She would forget people like Rory and his friends, who had all sucked her dry. Any liaisons she enjoyed in Tenerife would be casual and fun and conducted solely on her terms, while she concentrated on making a success of the Alcaszar project.

Later, she had studied the papers from the meeting and then eaten a solitary supper of cold meats and salad followed by a mouthwatering papaya. She didn't think she would ever get used to being able to buy such ripe, freshly picked, exotic fruit from the market, and she savored every juicy mouthful.

Now, fully rested after a second night of almost dreamless sleep, she was eager to get started. Exhilarated by the novelty of a short walk to the office in bright, early-morning sunshine, she pushed open the unlocked door with a cheery greeting.

There was nobody there. Conchita's desk was clear of paper,

and her chair was neatly tucked away. Matt's office door was open, and his desk was littered with papers, but there was no sign of him. Nor was Rufino anywhere to be seen.

Eager to get started, she wandered into Matt's office to look again at the photos and the plan of the Alcaszar that were fixed to the wall. It was built in the most spectacular setting, high up on a hillside, and in colors that matched the veins of creamy pink that seamed the dark volcanic rock.

She recalled what Matt had told her over their meal with Cristina and Rufino. He had said that it had been built at the time that Tenerife first found fame as a holiday destination and, in its day, had been a much sought-after luxury hotel. Then, as rental apartments and time-shares became popular, it had fallen on hard times, mainly because its owners had failed to keep up with the expectations of modern tourists. Slowly its flow of visitors had been reduced to a trickle, and by the time the owners had noticed, it was too late. Their finances failed, and unable to find a buyer, they had eventually cut their losses and left the Alcaszar to stand deserted and unloved for many years.

Regarded by many people as an outdated folly, there had been calls for it to be demolished before Matt rescued it. Sure that it had untapped potential, he had ignored Rufino's more conservative concerns and approached the local planning department with an offer it couldn't refuse. Now he had ten months to make it work. Ten months before the busy Christmas season started, because that was when he would need to recoup his money big-time if Miguel & Anderson were to profit from his gamble.

Alex was so intent on the plans as she attempted to build up a three-dimensional picture of the hotel in her head that she failed to hear Matt return. Nor did he realize that she had arrived, because she was hidden from view behind his office door. It was only when she turned away from the plans that she saw him. He was gazing out the window with his back to the room, a plastic cup of takeaway coffee in one hand. The end of a ham roll protruded from a white paper bag on his desk.

She opened her mouth to speak but stopped when she noticed

the slump of weary dejection about his shoulders and the shadow of yesterday's stubble on his cheek. He looked so lonely and vulnerable that she wished she hadn't come into his office but had waited at her own desk until he arrived. This felt like an intrusion, as if she were seeing a part of him that he kept hidden from the world. Perhaps she could tiptoe out without him noticing her.

But even as she had the thought, he swung round. It was almost as if he had felt her staring at him. Their eyes met, hers green and clear from a good night's sleep, his shadowed and tired, their striking blueness muted to a misty gray. For a long, long moment neither of them spoke. Eventually Alex broke the silence.

"I'm sorry," she stammered, her face flushed and her heart beating unaccountably fast. Her feeling of confusion was not helped by the brooding expression in his eyes as he continued to look at her. "I didn't hear you come in. I was too intent on the Alcaszar."

Her words were like a magic charm. Although he didn't smile, he straightened up and ran his fingers through his tousled hair, trying to tame it. His eyes lost their dullness, so that even the shadows seemed to fade as he walked across the room to stand with her before the photos and drawings that covered the wall. Together they stared at them.

"Well, what do you think?" His voice was friendly with no trace of the embarrassment that she felt. "Do you think my ideas are tenable, or am I deluding myself with what will turn out to be a white elephant?"

"I think it could be, um . . . wonderful . . . but . . ." She searched for the right words while keeping her eyes firmly fixed on the line drawings in front of her.

"But what?"

"I don't know if your ideas are possible in the time frame. Ten months is not very long."

"All the more reason to get started, then." He gave a short, impatient laugh that held little humor. "I'll take you up to the site straightaway so that you can see what we're faced with."

Sure that she had already fallen short of his expectations by introducing even the smallest doubt, Alex pretended to continue to study the plan while he swallowed the last of his coffee and searched for his car keys. She felt mean and silently berated herself for her negativity. Why hadn't she kept her mouth shut? Although she was here in a professional capacity and so was honor bound to give a professional opinion, a little leeway wouldn't have hurt this early in the project. After all, it was obvious that the Alcaszar was the one thing that made him forget painful memories, so the least she could have done was go along with it until she had seen the building.

"Ready?" He stood in the doorway, a thick file under his arm, his car keys dangling from one finger. The ham roll, still in its paper bag, lay ignored on his desk.

She turned toward him, wondering as she did so if he had had any sleep at all. His navy T-shirt was crumpled, and despite his best efforts with his fingers, his hair still looked as if he had stepped straight from his bed. Nor did she think the designer stubble was deliberate, but more an oversight from someone who had not looked into the mirror this morning. It must be terrible, she thought, to be so wrapped up in memories that the normal order of life fails. Although she had had to learn the hard way that Rory was wrong for her, she had eventually seen him for what he was and got over it. She had even moved on to the point where she could relish the sort of promise that she had seen in Francesco Pascual's eyes when they collided yesterday. But Matt was in another category entirely. To love someone as much as he must have loved his wife, and then to lose her, was a tragedy of such terrible proportions that she couldn't imagine how anyone would ever get over it.

"I'm ready," she said as she slipped past him to collect a notebook and pen from the pile of stationery that Conchita had placed on her desk. Then, looking up at him, she added in what she hoped was a conciliatory tone, "I'm really looking forward to seeing the Alcaszar after hearing so much about it. Take no notice of my concerns about completion, because I don't have any rights in that area until I've seen it."

"That doesn't mean that you're wrong," he conceded as they made their way along the narrow road and then down a flight of steps to a small parking lot. "I know we'll have our work cut out for us to be ready on time, but I owe it to Rufino to try, because I really went out on a limb with this one, and I can't let myself even begin to think about what might happen if we fail."

Alex aimed for a positive rejoinder as they walked toward his car, but it remained un-uttered, as someone called her name. She turned to see a tall, dark figure hurrying to catch up with them. It was Francesco. He looked cool and elegant in a white linen suit. He greeted them both cheerfully and then seized her hand and kissed it.

"You are even more beautiful today, Señorita Alexandra," he said, his black eyes bold and appraising as they looked her up and down. Unsure how to dress for work in a climate of almost perpetual sunshine, Alex had finally teamed a cream-colored silk top that did a lot for her figure without revealing too much flesh with a pair of green linen slacks and matching high-heeled sandals. Now, faced with the treacherous pavements, she wasn't so sure about the sandals, but she did know that she looked cool and professional.

"Thank you." Her cheeks flushed slightly as she tried, in vain, to withdraw her hand. "Matt and I are on our way to visit a development site."

"Ah, the famous Alcaszar, no doubt! Is the señorita to be another disciple?" There was a derogatory note in Francesco's voice as he turned to Matt, although his charm remained intact.

"I guess that's up to Alex. I'm afraid we're in a bit of a hurry, though, so if you'll excuse us . . ." Matt's voice was curt as he moved forward, effectively breaking the clasp of Francesco's hand.

"Of course! Forgive me!" The tall Spaniard stood back with a half smile on his face. He didn't look remotely contrite. As they moved away, he called after them.

"I will find you again, Señorita Alexandra, when you have

more time. And then I will introduce you to the delights of Tenerife."

Alex flashed him a smile but didn't reply as she waved farewell. She did, however, cast a surreptitious look at Matt's set face from beneath her eyelashes. Surely she hadn't really heard him mutter "Over my dead body" under his breath, had she? What was going on here?

Matt remained silent until they had driven out of the parking lot and onto the main road leading to the Alcaszar. Alex sat beside him, still too bemused by his behavior to think of anything to say. It wasn't until they had negotiated a roundabout and were traveling uphill that he spoke, and then, without any preamble and without looking at her, he began to question her.

"When did you meet him?" he said.

"Francesco?"

"Yes, Francesco! Assuming of course that you haven't yet been here long enough to meet the rest of the local lotharios!"

She felt her temper flare. How dare he speak to her like that! And what was it to him, anyway? Her life outside the office was her own, so it was none of his business if she chose to meet up with Francesco or anyone else who interested her. With difficulty she bit back an angry retort, but her irritation was apparent in her voice as she answered him.

"I collided with him yesterday, and he spilled the books he was carrying all over the road. We introduced ourselves while we picked them up, and he told me that he is related to Cristina. She says that he's fun," she added defiantly.

"If fun is what you want, then I'm sure Cristina is right." Matt sounded so dismissive that she glanced at him just as he slowed down for a traffic light. He looked across at her at the same moment, and their eyes met and held for a second time that morning, but this time his were the color of a summer storm, and his mouth was grim.

"He's a very distant relative, not someone she spends much time with. Francesco Pascual is a lightweight and a womanizer and not to be trusted."

"I think I'm experienced enough to judge such matters for myself," Alex said stiffly. "I'm hardly a child, nor am I looking for anything more than a casual friendship. This is not a life-or-death thing, you know!"

As soon as the words left her mouth she felt sick and ashamed. How crass! How insensitive of her to mention life and death! Whatever the provocation, she should have chosen her words more carefully. He was probably just looking out for her because she worked for Tom. She knew that their friendship went back a long way. Contrite, she put her hand on his forearm, where it rested against the steering wheel.

"I'm sorry. I don't mean to sound ungrateful for your advice, but I really can manage my own social life, you know."

That's what she intended to say, and that's what she hoped came out of her mouth, but suddenly she wasn't sure, because in the space of two seconds she lost all sense of reality as the warmth of his bare arm under her hand produced a most unexpected sensation. One moment she was trying to defuse a situation that seemed to have come from nowhere, and the next she found breathing almost impossible as a shivery feeling traveled from her fingertips to her throat, leaving her senses spinning and her pulse in overdrive. She pulled her hand away as if she had been stung.

Whatever was happening to her? That was twice in the space of twenty minutes that she had reacted like a silly schoolgirl. Surely she couldn't be attracted to Matthew Anderson. That was just ridiculous! For a start, he wasn't her type. He was too moody, too serious, too . . . She tried desperately to think of some more negatives without success. And anyway, what was her type? She'd once thought that outgoing, charismatic Rory was right for her and had been proved oh so wrong.

Dismayed by the direction of her thoughts, she gave herself a mental shaking. This was ridiculous. She would stick to her plan. She liked Francesco's style. The admiration in his eyes was good for her ego. Also, she knew without being told that he wasn't serious relationship material. No, Francesco would offer just the sort of casual friendship that she had deliberately

decided would herald her reentry into the world of dating.
Nothing heavy. Just some fun on an island made for enjoyment.

Matt wasn't even available, for goodness' sake. He was a
widower whose grief seemed to be such that he couldn't even
bear to be alone in his own house anymore. He was someone
who immersed himself in his work so that he didn't need to
think. She identified with that, of course, because, in a small
way, she had experienced it herself after Rory left her, so she
knew only too well that work could be a real lifesaver. That
had to be it, she decided, tucking her hand firmly into her lap.
She was just mistaking her feelings of sympathy for something stronger.

Matt pushed his foot down too hard on the accelerator as her
hand sent electric shocks up his arm. His action forced him to
concentrate on the narrow road winding up above the town.
Anything to stop thinking about the cool touch of her fingers,
anything to stop that out-of-control feeling that had started
again, despite his best intentions, as soon as he had set eyes on
her again this morning.

After two almost sleepless nights, one of which had been
spent sprawled across the bed fully dressed, he was still no
nearer to understanding why she affected him this way. He
had taken out prettier girls. He had taken out sexier girls. In
fact, before his marriage he had played the field almost as
thoroughly as Francesco Pascual without ever reacting this
way. Only with his wife had he come close. Close, but not the
same, because his initial attraction to Adriana now seemed an
insubstantial thing compared with this connection with Alex
that was like nothing he had ever experienced before. He
didn't need her to touch his arm to set his pulse racing. Just
watching her smile was enough for his stomach to start up the
backflips again. And he didn't know how to deal with it.

After twenty-four hours of agonizing he had almost persuaded himself that he was in control, until he fell asleep and
dreamed about her. Although it was a shadowy and elusive
dream that had fled the instant he awoke, he nevertheless

knew with utter certainty that during the night he had lost the battle, and he succumbed to a feeling of total despair at what was happening to him. He couldn't go through it again! Couldn't cope with the emotional highs and lows, couldn't cope with the inevitable loss. He had to find a way out of this.

It had been half an hour before he had summoned enough energy to drag himself off the bed. Then he had discovered that he had run out of coffee and bread. Without bothering to shower or shave, he had unlocked the office door and gone out in search of sustenance.

When he returned to the office, he had stood by the window drinking his coffee while trying to decide how best to manage the situation. Should he get Rufino to take Alex to the site? And while she worked on the Alcaszar project, would he be able to find sufficient ways of distancing himself from her to make his working life bearable? Because, however much his treacherous body wanted him to, he had no intention of making any sort of move toward her. Even without his own emotional hang-ups, it wouldn't work. She was too intent on having fun. Her description of her life in London had made that abundantly clear. Besides, she would return to the UK in six months' time, to London and to her high-powered job. It was clear that she was ambitious, and he knew that she was good. Tom had sent him an e-mail telling him that he was sending him one of his best designers. He had just failed to explain that she was female.

It was as he was thinking these thoughts that he had felt a shiver down his spine and a sensation that when he turned around she would be in the room with him. Feeling ridiculous, he had swung around and found himself looking into startled green eyes. He had stared at her speechlessly, wondering for one mad moment if his thoughts had caused her to materialize like a genie from a lamp. Then she had broken the spell with a stammering apology that had forced him to pull himself together with a wry smile at such fanciful thoughts.

After that he had tried to behave normally, although admittedly without much success. He knew that his behavior this morning had been fairly eccentric, to say the least. He had been abrupt. He had been rude. He had spoken out of turn. And, he realized, as he caught a glimpse of himself in the driving mirror, he still hadn't shaved! Nor had he showered or put on fresh clothes. He looked tired and scruffy. Well, at least that solved one problem. Whatever he felt about Alex, she certainly wasn't going to be interested in the spectacle that he was presenting, not with someone as smooth and elegant as Francesco Pascual to pay her attention.

Neither of them spoke again until the Alcaszar came into view. Alex saw it as they rounded the final bend in a road that kept climbing ever more steeply toward it. Built into the hillside, it blended into its surroundings so that it looked as if it had been carved out of the volcanic rock itself. Creamy pink, with sharply pitched towers, long, high windows, and crenellated surrounding walls, it was like something out of a child's storybook. The effect was heightened by overgrown gardens where giant weeds battled with riotous plants, many of them clambering over trees and bushes or twining around the elegant trunks of windswept palms. It was so unexpected and magical that she could almost believe there might be a princess asleep in the topmost turret.

"It's a fairy-tale castle!" she blurted out, and then was embarrassed that she was capable of such an unprofessional statement. Even as she spoke, she recognized that its design was loosely based on the Moorish architecture still common in much of Spain.

Matt's smile at her obvious delight wiped some of the tension and tiredness from his face. "In that case, I guess you are the good fairy here to rescue it," he said. "I just hope that you can concoct enough spells while you're over here to bring it back to life."

He drove through the gateway as he spoke, past a weathered sign and a pile of broken garden furniture, and brought the car to a halt at what appeared to be the main entrance.

"Come on. Come and see what you've let yourself in for."

He produced a key and proceeded to unlock a huge wooden door set into an elaborate archway. Pushing it open, he went inside.

Alex followed him into an echoing foyer with sweeping stalactite vaulting. Despite the grandeur of the design, it was so dim and dusty that she could barely see, until Matt began to open doors hidden in the gloom. Then it suddenly became alive with garish color. Beams of sunlight lit the walls and highlighted the deep reds and purples that fought with yellows and blues in a riot of geometric designs that covered every inch of plasterwork. In contrast the floor was a dull brown, as was the wooden paneling that surrounded what had obviously once been a reception desk.

"Don't stop," Matt commanded, chuckling at the horrified expression on her face. "You have to get past this bit to appreciate the real wonders of the Alcaszar."

Hoping that he was right, Alex crossed the hall to where he was standing beside yet another door. This one was closed.

"Close your eyes," he said, holding out his hand. Without thinking, she curled her fingers into his. He opened the door, and she let him lead her through, telling herself that the warmth that was flowing up her arm and down toward her heart was only a reaction to his excitement as he shared his dream with her.

"Now you can open them." Matt placed his free hand on her shoulder as he spoke and turned her slightly away from him so that she could fully appreciate the scene that unfolded before her as she opened her eyes.

She stared about her in amazement. They were standing in a walled courtyard surrounded by horseshoe-shaped arches on slim white columns. In the center was a dry fountain carved from white marble. A repeat of the garish geometric designs that she had seen in the foyer decorated the panels above the arches, but even this failed to spoil its grace and beauty.

"It's incredible," she said, gazing about her. "It's like something from a film set." She was so enthralled by her surroundings that for a long moment she forgot she was still holding his hand.

Matt glanced down at her with conflicting emotions as he watched her expression. So far her reaction to the Alcaszar was all he could have asked for. He was sure that once she had viewed it all, she would share his dream. He could see it in the burgeoning excitement on her face. Yet he derived little satisfaction from it, because he knew that each moment of shared commitment would carry a bittersweet aftertaste. However much he wished otherwise, dreams were all they could ever share, because it was going to be a long, long time before he was ready to invite somebody else into his life. With an inward sigh he gently extricated his fingers from her warm clasp and moved away from her, calling himself all kinds of a fool as he felt momentarily bereft.

His action returned Alex to the here and now. She had been so entranced by the walled courtyard, and so lost in contemplation as her designer's eye considered possibilities, that she had forgotten Matt. But when he dropped her hand, she was jerked back into an awareness of their intimacy. The warmth of his palm against hers persisted as she took in the fact that they were alone together in what had to be one of the most romantic settings on the island. She needed to do something with her hands, anything to return everything to normal. Without looking at him she delved into her capacious shoulder bag and pulled out the pen and notepad she had stashed there earlier.

"I'm going to look at the rest of the hotel," she said as briskly as she could. "This is lovely, but we'll need more than one courtyard to sell the hotel to the discriminating tourist."

"I guess." He nodded his agreement. "Shall I come with you, or would you rather view it on your own?"

"Oh, I'll be fine on my own, if you have other things to do," Alex replied, striving for a nonchalance she didn't feel. "It will take me quite a while, so don't let me keep you."

He hesitated. Surely he shouldn't leave her here alone. If she had an accident, it was too remote, too isolated. And yet he knew that the building was safe. He had surveyed every inch of it, and it was as sound as a bell. She couldn't come to any harm, and he really didn't have the time to spend hours waiting for her. The Alcaszar had taken so much of his attention recently that the lion's share of Miguel & Anderson's bread-and-butter business had fallen to Rufino, and he felt bad about it. Now that Alex was here, he could put that right while at the same time giving her the time and space she needed to come up with an interior design.

"I do have things to do if you're sure you'll be okay," he admitted. "You can call me on your cell phone if you have any problems, and I'll drive back to collect you whenever you're ready."

Suddenly Alex wanted him gone. She wanted to be able to concentrate on the Alcaszar without the distraction of his presence. Already she felt good about its potential, but she needed to be sure, and that would be difficult to achieve with Matt two steps behind her. There would be time enough in the next six months to think about why he affected her so. Right now all she wanted to do was get on with the job at hand, the job she was being paid to do.

"I'll be fine," she told him. "Please don't worry about me. I'll call you when I'm ready."

Chapter Six

Once she was alone, Alex began to walk slowly around the courtyard, filling it with imaginary items as she did so. In her mind's eye it became a place of light and shade. She soothed the lurid décor into warm pastels, painted the slim columns with fresh white paint, and introduced wooden tables and chairs and large urns of exotic flowers, making these its only decoration apart from the foaming fountain, which she would return to its former glory.

Then, after allowing herself another moment to savor it, she moved purposefully back toward the entrance and began a systematic tour of the whole building, making copious notes on a set of plans that Matt had left with her. It took her a long time, and by the time she reached the topmost tower, she was thirsty and her feet were aching. She sat on the low stone windowsill, kicked off her shoes, and wriggled her toes. She really must stop this stupid predilection for ridiculously high heels. They might help her forget her lack of inches, they might make her legs look longer and slimmer, but they didn't make her working day comfortable. She should have realized she was going to visit the Alcaszar today and worn something more sensible. She should also have put a bottle of water in her bag.

She stretched and leaned back against the wall, and then, turning her head, she looked out the window. The view was incredible. In the far distance the sea glinted blue and green in the sun. Boats, as small as matchboxes from this distance, bobbed about on the waves. Closer in she could see dark shadows where rocks crouched just beneath the water, and she watched, fascinated, as an occasional wave, larger than the rest, curled across the gray-green depths to break against them in a plume of milky spray.

From her vantage point she felt as if she was at the prow of a great ship, far away from land, adrift on the ocean. For a while she sat, soothed by the gentle swell of water that stretched as far as she could see, but then she began to feel hungry as well as thirsty. The time had come to call Matt.

With a sigh she reached into her bag for her cell phone. It wasn't there. She searched again and then emptied the entire contents of her bag onto the windowsill. No sign of it. Somehow she must have dropped it during her exploration.

She racked her brain. When had she last opened her bag? Was it when she had looked for a highlighter pen, or when she had needed a tissue because the dust in some of the unused rooms had made her sneeze? She couldn't remember, and anyway, speculation was useless. There were too many rooms and too many stairs. She could have dropped it anywhere.

Cursing under her breath, she picked up her shoes and started the long trek down to the ground floor on bare feet. Although she tried to retrace her steps as much as possible, she didn't find her phone. Disconsolately she slipped her aching feet back into her shoes and wandered out to the beautiful courtyard. She would just have to wait until Matt arrived. He was bound to return eventually.

Caught up in meetings and paperwork, it was the middle of the afternoon before Matt glanced at his watch. He frowned when he saw how late it was. Surely Alex had finished by now. He had only intended that she should stay long enough to familiarize herself with the layout of the Alcaszar and perhaps begin to get a feel for possible color schemes and décor. He had anticipated it would be little more than a couple of hours before she called to ask him to collect her.

He looked up as Conchita came into his office carrying a mug of coffee and moved papers aside so that she could put it on his desk.

"Have you eaten anything today?" she asked, poking suspiciously at the ham roll, still in its paper bag but now dry and hard.

He ignored her, too intent on checking his cell phone for missed calls. There weren't any.

"Have you heard from Alex?"

"No." She caught the concern in his voice. "Would you like me to call her?"

When he nodded, she returned to the outer office. Five minutes later she was back.

"She's not answering."

Matt took a quick gulp of his coffee as he pushed his chair away from the desk. "Then I'd better drive back to the Alcaszar in case she's in trouble. If she calls, let me know."

Looking at the papers scattered across his desk and the third mug of coffee that he had failed to finish that day, Conchita sighed. Then she shrugged and returned to her desk. She had her own work to do, and she had long ago given up trying to fathom Matthew Anderson. He was far too buttoned-up for her taste.

Driving back up the twisting road to the Alcaszar, Matt was feeling far from buttoned-up as his emotions veered sharply between worry and anger. What if something had happened to Alex? It would be entirely his fault for leaving her on her own. On the other hand, maybe she had made other arrangements, called up someone else to collect her, gone out to lunch with them, and just not bothered to let him know. He didn't think such a thing was beyond the realm of possibility, given the speed at which she had made contact with Francesco Pascual. If her stories of her life in London were anything to go by, then she was obviously someone who liked a good time. So maybe she had just given the Alcaszar a cursory once-over and then hightailed it back into town for a leisurely lunch. Despite himself, he didn't really believe that, though, and with his foot hard on the gas pedal and his jaw clenched, he made it back to the hotel in record time.

Arriving at the main entrance, he jumped from the driver's seat and, without bothering to close the car door behind him, hurried into the hotel calling Alex's name as he did so. There was no sign of her anywhere. He strode from room to room and then from floor to floor, taking the stairs two at a time until he reached the topmost tower. Nothing! He pulled his cell from his pocket and speed dialed her number. No answer! He tried again, and suddenly he heard a faint ring tone. He followed the sound until he found Alex's cell phone in one of the bedrooms, half hidden under a pile of forgotten curtains.

By now thoroughly alarmed, he retraced his steps until he stood at the hotel entrance. Where could she be? Had someone surprised her and made her drop her cell, or had she just lost it? Something scuffed his foot as he moved forward, and he looked down. Her leather shoulder bag was lying just inside the door. It was half open, and the contents were spilling out.

An icy coldness in the pit of his stomach galvanized Matt into swift action. He ran to where the lounge and dining areas opened onto a wide terrace that overlooked the gardens. Fitting a key to one of the glass casements, he flung it open and stepped outside. From the edge of the terrace he could see the whole vista of the gardens in all their overgrown glory. He shaded his eyes from the sun as he searched in vain for any sign of Alex.

There was nowhere else to look. The terrace stretched around three of the four sides of the hotel, with only the front entrance excluded. Calling her name, he walked the length of the terrace again and then again, unable to believe that she had just disappeared into thin air. Finally, cursing fluently and repeatedly, he vaulted the stone balustrade, landed in a tangle of weeds, and began to make his way through the lush greenery, hoping against hope that he would find that she had merely fallen asleep under a tree.

When he did find her, close to the overgrown path but half hidden by a low-growing bush that, chameleonlike, mirrored the cream and green of her clothes, he thought for the briefest moment that she was asleep. Her eyes were closed, certainly, but on closer examination she didn't look comfortable. Her body was lying at an awkward angle, and her face was smeared with earth. With an exclamation of concern he moved forward.

Alex opened her eyes and looked up at him. Silhouetted against the sun, he seemed impossibly tall from where she was lying, and she couldn't see his face against the glare. She knew it was Matt, though.

"You took your time," she mumbled through dry lips as she struggled to sit up.

Seeing her wince, Matt knelt down beside her and supported her shoulders with his arm. Her face was smeared, and her hands and nails were dirty, as if she had been scrabbling in the soil.

"Whatever happened?" he asked, conjuring up all sorts of tortured scenes in his mind. "Has someone attacked you? When I found your cell phone in one of the bedrooms and your bag lying open near the door, I thought you'd been abducted or something worse."

"Nothing so melodramatic." Alex gave him the vestige of a shamefaced smile. "I dropped my cell phone somewhere in the hotel, which meant that I couldn't call you to say I'd finished, so I decided to investigate the garden while I waited for you to return. I left my bag by the door so you'd know I was still around. What is so stupid is that I kept to the paths because I thought they would be safe. Unfortunately, I didn't anticipate loose flagstones. A few of them are very unstable. There's a gaping hole underneath one section, probably dug by an animal. My foot sort of twisted when my heel disappeared into the gap between the stones, which is why those will never be the same again!" She nodded ruefully toward a pair of green sling-back sandals lying on the grass beside her. One no longer had a heel, and both shoes were now the worse for wear, their leather uppers scraped and soiled with streaks of dirt.

Matt looked at them in disbelief. The thin heels had to be four inches high, and she had thought she was safe wandering along weed-strewn paths in them, to say nothing of the creeping vines lying in wait for the unwary.

"How could you be so . . . ," he began, fright and guilt making him angry with her. He knew that it wasn't really her fault, because one of the building contractors had already warned him about the flagstones and told him to cordon them off. He had intended to, but there were always too many things demanding his attention, so that, without meaning to, he had kept pushing them to the bottom of his problem pile. He wondered how long it would take him to organize a team of landscapers. He would get on it as soon as they returned to the office. Then he noticed Alex's pallor and the awkward way she was holding herself, and he bit off the rest of his accusation.

"Where have you hurt yourself?"

"Mainly my ankle," she admitted, relieved that he no longer seemed about to throttle her. "And my shoulder a bit as well."

"Can you stand?"

"I don't think so. I tried to pull myself up when I fell, but it hurt so much that I think I fainted. When I came to, I decided the best option was to lie still until you came back."

Inwardly chastising himself for having left her alone for so long, he slipped his arms under her shoulders and knees and lifted her up without a word and with barely a grunt of effort. Then, with infinite care, he picked his way along the path that had been her undoing and carried her back to his car.

Despite wincing as an occasional movement jarred her shoulder or a dangling branch caught at her ankle, Alex almost forgot her injuries as she became aware of the rapid pounding of Matt's heart against her rib cage and saw the pulse beating fast at the base of his throat. To her consternation her own heart seemed to be beating in unison. The warmth of his body, too, was having a peculiar effect, as was the fresh, lemony smell of his skin. Shower gel, she decided, trying to distract herself from more intimate thoughts. And he'd shaved, too, and changed.

Shifting her head a little, she saw that he was wearing a polo shirt the same bright blue as his eyes. She saw, too, that the unbuttoned collar exposed a strong brown throat and chest. As if he was aware of her scrutiny, Matt glanced down at her. He seemed unfazed by her weight as he climbed the steps to where his car was parked.

"Are you okay?"

"Yes. Thank you." She met his gaze, nodded, and then looked quickly away before he could notice the flush staining her cheeks. It must be proximity, she decided. That, together with her promise to herself to start dating again, meant that her hormones considered Matt eligible even though she knew he was not. And it had been a long, long time since anyone had held her so intimately.

It didn't finish when he helped her into the car either, because then he took her bare foot in his hands and examined her swollen ankle, moving it this way and that to gauge the severity of her injury, only stopping when she gave an involuntary cry of pain.

"I'm pretty sure that it's just a bad sprain," he said finally, his fingers firm against her leg as he rested her foot on his knee. "The best thing to do is get some ice on it as soon as possible, to reduce the swelling."

He placed her foot gently on the floor in front of the passenger seat and then leaned across and strapped her in, his fingers brushing across her thighs as he did so. Her eyes darkened as a sudden tingle of desire swept through her, and she was full of a growing confusion as she watched him return to the Alcaszar to collect her bag and lock up.

Ten minutes later they pulled up outside what appeared to be a heavy wooden gate set in an ancient stone wall. Matt climbed down from the car and went inside. Left to her own devices, Alex was mystified. Where were they? She had been too intent on cushioning the pain of her wrenched shoulder to notice that they were on a different road. Now, looking about her, she realized that they had driven deeper into the hills. Before she could speculate further, Matt reappeared, pulled open the passenger door, and picked her up again as if she were a child.

"I decided that driving to my house was an easier and much quicker journey for you than the twists and turns and stop-start traffic that returning to town would have involved," he said. "Besides, the sooner we tend to your injuries, the better."

He carried her through the gate and up some steps as he spoke, and then into a tiled courtyard where several tubs of scarlet geraniums stood next to a bright blue slatted bench. Twin lanterns were set on either side of the entrance, and a profusion of flowers grew in sloping beds beside the steps. The house itself, which was set farther back, was a sprawling, single-story building painted in shades of terra-cotta. Obviously old, it had large, irregularly shaped decorative stones set at random into the walls, which gave it a slightly rakish air. The front door was open, and Matt carried her through it and gently lowered her onto a pale gray sofa. Looking around, Alex saw that she was in a large room with wide picture windows and a magnificent view.

He disappeared into what she assumed was a kitchen, leaving her stranded on piled cushions. She was touched that he had put her comfort first and brought her to his own house instead of driving back to town, because she knew from Cristina how difficult it was for him to be here. She studied the room, wondering as she did so how often he came back. It looked well cared for and tidy, but like his crash pad above Miguel & Anderson, it gave nothing away. There were no flowers or ornaments, and no photos. There was nothing to show that he had ever had a wife, nothing to show that this had once been a real home.

He reappeared with a glass of orange juice and a freshly opened bottle of water. "Drink these while I sort out some painkillers and ice cubes. It must be hours since you drank anything."

She gulped the orange juice gratefully and began to feel marginally better as soon as it hit her bloodstream. Matt returned with a bowl of warm water, towels, a pack of ice, and the painkillers. He smiled for the first time.

"Here, you might want to clean yourself up while I look at your ankle."

She reached for her bag, which he had dumped on the floor beside her, and took out a hand mirror. Her face was smeared with dirt, and there were leaves and debris in her hair. Horrified by her bedraggled appearance, she tidied herself up as best she could, all the while trying to ignore the fact that Matt was holding her foot. By the time she had finished, he had elevated her leg on a pile of cushions and packed towels and ice around her ankle.

"That should do the trick. Now let me look at your shoulder."

He rested his fingers against her neck as he spoke, waiting for her to sit forward. Once she did so, he gently manipulated her upper arm and shoulder and then massaged the muscles at the base of her neck, all of which caused the oddest of reactions. First she felt as if her body were liquefying under the warmth of his touch. It was almost as if her bones and muscles were dissolving. Then, as his hands moved more firmly, she tensed so much that her shoulder went into some sort of spasm. She gasped at the sudden pain. Immediately he stopped.

"What did I do?" he asked, worried that he had missed something and that she had a more serious injury than he thought.

"Nothing." She shook her head. "It's really nothing. I just tensed up for some reason. It's okay now."

As she spoke, she looked up at him. Their eyes met and held for a moment before hers flickered away. If he had any idea that the intimacy of his touch had been the reason for her tense reaction, he didn't show it. Instead he just told her to make herself as comfortable as possible while he prepared some food.

Left to her own devices once again, Alex lay back against the cushions and closed her eyes. She wasn't going to think about Matt anymore. For one thing, she was too tired and, despite the painkillers, everything hurt. For another, she was too confused by her reaction to him to think straight.

* * *

She must have drifted off to sleep, because when she next opened her eyes, Matt had moved a low table next to the sofa and was standing over her holding a tray.

"Can you manage to sit up?" he asked.

She hauled herself up from the soft comfort of the cushions and took the tray. On it was another glass of orange juice, two rolls, a bright yellow omelette, and a green salad.

He stuffed two more cushions behind her to support her back and then sat in the chair opposite with a tray of his own.

The food was good, and Alex, surprisingly ravenous in spite of the trauma of her afternoon, didn't take long to do it justice.

"That was absolutely delicious," she told him as she finished the last mouthful.

"All courtesy of my neighbors," he said. "I let them use part of the garden to grow vegetables, so I always have salad on tap, and eggs, too, because they keep chickens and ducks. So what with that and the freezer I am never without basic food however long I stay away."

Alex looked across the room at the view, disappearing now into the rapidly growing dusk. From the little she could see, the house itself appeared to be surrounded by trees and grass, while in the distance a forest climbed up the side of a mountain.

"I don't know how you can bear to be away from it at all. It's so beautiful. I don't think I've ever been anywhere so peaceful and quiet."

He rose to his feet abruptly as she spoke and took her tray. He didn't answer her but merely muttered something about making coffee and disappeared. To her chagrin she found herself wishing for the second time that day that she had watched her words more carefully. It was obvious from his reaction that his lovely home still held such unbearable memories that he couldn't even acknowledge its beauty. She hoped it would be easier in the future when the passing of time had blurred the edges of his loss.

Later, after coffee, Alex found that she could hardly keep her eyes open. Tired out by the travails of the day, all she wanted to do was sleep. With an effort she stirred herself and suggested that they should make a move. Matt shook his head.

"Not a good idea. A bumpy journey down the mountain at this time of night will undo all the healing we've achieved. You're looking much better now that you've eaten and rested. The color is back in your cheeks, and you don't appear to be in so much discomfort. Stay here tonight, and I'll call Cristina in the morning and ask her to bring you a change of clothes."

Part of her could think of nothing better. The thought of snuggling into the sofa cushions and drifting off to sleep seemed the most desirable thing in the world; but deep inside her a small voice advised caution. It kept reminding her of how much Matt's continuing presence disturbed her, even though he seemed to be totally unaware of it, and how much more she would have to rely on him if she were to sleep in his house for the night.

"I can't put you to that sort of trouble," she protested, knowing as she said it that it was a weak excuse. After all, from his point of view, staying at the house for the night was less trouble than asking him to drive her back down the twisting mountain road to her apartment, to say nothing of the fact that he would probably have to carry her out to the car again.

"No trouble." He shook his head, quite obviously impatient with her logic. "I have four spare beds, and the woman who looks after the house for me always keeps them freshly made up, so you can take your pick. Besides, I feel responsible for your accident. I knew the path was unstable, and I should have done something about it, so the least you can do is let me take care of you until tomorrow. That way I won't feel quite so guilty."

For the briefest moment the independent side of Alex wanted to insist that he take her home, but then she recognized how churlish that would be. Besides, if he was prepared to spend the night at the one place he most eschewed just so she could recover from her ordeal, then the least she could do was be grateful. She didn't go down without a fight, though.

"Let me sleep on the sofa, then," she suggested. "It's very comfortable, and I'll be fine as I am."

He hesitated, apparently not wanting to coerce her, but then he gave another, more decisive shake of his head. "No. You need a proper night's sleep. Besides, if you stay in here, I'll disturb you if I get up early."

He crossed the room as he spoke and gently lowered her legs to the floor. To her relief, her ankle was far less painful. "I think I can manage to walk a little," she said.

He didn't bother to answer her. Instead he just swung her up into his arms and carried her through the house to where the bedrooms were situated. He deposited her on the bed in one of them with an apologetic smile.

"Sorry about manhandling you, but the less you put your foot to the ground, the better. This bedroom has an en suite, so everything you need is within hobble distance."

Dampening down the pulse that had started going haywire again as soon as he touched her, she smiled shyly back at him, suddenly grateful all over again for his concern and sorry that she had put him to so much trouble. He didn't give her time to thank him, though. Instead he left the room to collect towels, extra pillows, and a neatly folded T-shirt. He dropped these onto the bed and then, promising her more painkillers once she was ready for sleep, he left her to it.

Gingerly she put her foot to the floor. It was marginally better. Hopping and hobbling, she made her way to the bathroom and with only a little difficulty managed to undress and get ready for bed. Ten minutes later she was tucked between cool cotton sheets, watching the movement of the ruffled curtains as they wafted slowly to and fro in the slight breeze from the window.

Matt, tapping at the bedroom door five minutes later, was concerned when there was no reply. He waited for a few moments and then tried again. Finally he opened the door. Alex was already asleep, her long hair braided into a single plait that fell across one shoulder, her face cushioned on her hand. He stared down at her for a long time before placing a glass of water and a bottle of painkillers on the bedside table. Then he pulled the curtains, turned out the light, and crept silently from the room.

He spent the next fifteen minutes clearing up their supper things. Then he poured himself a very large glass of whiskey and took it to a small terrace overlooking the nearby hills, where he sat for a very long time staring sightlessly into the darkness of the night.

Chapter Seven

Alex woke in the early hours of the morning, uncomfortably aware of the throbbing in her ankle. For the briefest moment she wondered where she was, but then everything came flooding back to her as she reached out and switched on the bedside light. Seeing pills and water on the table, she realized that Matt must have come into the room while she was asleep, and she was filled with embarrassment at the thought of such an intimate action. Somehow her plan to work hard and play hard while keeping all emotional involvement at bay seemed to be falling about her ears before it had even begun.

With a sigh she swallowed the painkillers and, recognizing that she was unlikely to fall asleep again very quickly, used her one good arm to plump up the pillows behind her head. She looked around the room. All the furniture was carved pine, and the sprigged and ruffled curtains and bedcovers reflected the cream and blue bathroom, as did the square rug on the pale, tiled floor. It was a pretty room with a distinctly feminine touch. It was also the only thing that she had seen in the house so far that gave any indication at all that a woman had ever lived there. Had Matt's wife decorated it? she wondered. Had she chosen the rug, picked out the covers at a local store, or even sent away for them?

Alex wished she could know more about her, what sort of person she had been, how she had lived her life. She looked around for more clues, but there was nothing. She turned her attention to the bedside table and, after a brief moment of hesitation, slid open the drawer. It was full of magazines.

She lifted them out with her good arm and saw that they were outdated women's magazines. Unfortunately they were in Spanish, so she could only flick through the photos, picking out the occasional word when something of interest caught her eye. Did that mean that Matt's wife had been Spanish? It was highly likely, she supposed, because he seemed to have lived on Tenerife for a number of years.

Shifting to a more comfortable position, she inadvertently tipped most of the magazines onto the floor. Irritated by her clumsiness, she leaned from the bed and, with considerable difficulty, picked them up one by one and stacked them on the bedside table. At the bottom of the pile she found loose papers and a couple of envelopes. She picked those up too. As she did so, a photograph fell from one of the envelopes. It was a formal head-and-shoulders shot of a stunning, dark-haired girl with sparkling black eyes and a seductive smile. Although her long hair was twisted into a chignon, wispy curls snaked at her temples and the base of her neck, giving her a distinctly sultry air. Her makeup looked as if it had been professionally applied. A deep red lipstick enhanced full lips, while skillful brush-strokes of blusher and eye shadow exaggerated the exotic beauty of the rest of her face. Alex turned it over. Across the back a message was scrawled in a bold hand: *Mateo—nunca olvídese de mí. Adriana.*

Frowning, she tried to decipher it. *Mateo* was obviously Spanish for "Matthew." *Nunca* meant "never." She stared at the writing as she tried to remember Spanish lessons from high school. Suddenly it came to her: *Matthew—never forget me. Adriana.* So his wife had been called Adriana. Well, she'd certainly gotten her wish. He couldn't forget her.

Alex looked at the woman in the photo again and knew that she would never be able to compete with the memory of someone so vibrant and beautiful; not that she was going to have to, of course, because it was very clear that Matt wasn't in the market for any sort of relationship. So however much her wayward body reacted to his touch, however much his penetrating blue-eyed regard filled her with confusion, she was just going to have to stick with her original plan and concentrate on the obviously available Francesco Pascual.

In the next room Matt was experiencing his third sleepless night in a row, when he heard a slight thud through the wall. For a moment he wondered if Alex was okay. Then he gave an impatient sigh. Of course she was all right. She wasn't a child. He turned onto his side and stared at stars that were now beginning to fade against a slowly creeping dawn. What was he going to do?

Although he had managed to keep his emotions damped down for much of the previous day, he was under no illusion about his feelings for Alex. He wanted her with an urgency that had nothing to do with the long months of his self-imposed celibacy. He wondered if she felt the same. That electric shock as their hands met, the fast beating of his heart as he lifted her in his arms; surely he wasn't the only one experiencing such reactions. Nor was her attraction just physical. There was something else about her that his ragged emotions responded to: a sharp intelligence, an innate kindness, and something else, a sense of vulnerability despite her professional coolness. He was sure he hadn't imagined the shadow that had darkened her eyes or the quickly controlled quiver of her body as he tended to her injuries. His instincts told him that there was more to her than she was prepared to show to the world.

Suddenly he gave a soft, humorless laugh, threw back his bedcovers, and got out of bed. Who was he kidding? To date, reliance on his instincts had resulted in one totally screwed-up life, and if he valued his future sanity, that was something that he hadn't better forget in a hurry.

Alex heard Matt moving about and wondered if she should try to get up. She glanced at her watch. It wasn't even six o'clock; far too early for civilized conversation. Besides, she didn't want to spend any more time with him today than was necessary. It was too unsettling. It would be far better if she stayed in bed until Cristina arrived with some fresh clothes. That way she could avoid a repeat of their intimacy of the previous evening and return her relationship with Matt to a more professional footing.

When she looked at her watch again, she was surprised to see that it was eight o'clock. Despite herself, she had fallen asleep again and—so much for avoiding any intimate contact—Matt was tapping at her bedroom door.

"Breakfast's on its way," he called. "I'm just giving you time to make yourself decent."

He came into the bedroom a few minutes later carrying a tray laden with orange juice, melon, toast, and jam. He put it on the bedside table, frowning at the stack of magazines as he did so.

"I didn't know these were still here," he said, scooping them up. "I'll get rid of them, unless your Spanish is better than you say."

"It isn't," she admitted. "And I apologize for opening the drawer, but I was looking for something to read during the night while I waited for the painkillers to work."

He moved toward the door, the magazines bunched under his arm. "How are your injuries this morning?"

"Much better, thank you. I'll be back at work in no time."

He nodded his approval. "Good. I thought a bit of enforced rest would do the trick. Now, eat your breakfast while I make some coffee."

As she turned gratefully to the breakfast tray, a thought struck her.

"Matt."

He stopped in the doorway and turned to look at her.

"There's a photograph of a lovely woman in one of those envelopes. I didn't mean to pry. It fell out. It's just that . . . well, you might want to keep it." Her voice trailed off as she saw the grim expression on his face. Perhaps she had been wrong to bring it to his attention. After all, there were no other photos of Adriana anywhere in the house as far as she could tell.

When he answered her, however, his voice was pleasant enough, grateful even. It wasn't until much later, when she limped into the kitchen with her breakfast tray to brush toast crumbs and melon skin into the trash can, that she saw the photo again. And this time she stared at it in disbelief, because it had been torn into small pieces and was stained with the juice of discarded melon seeds.

She stood with the tray in her hands as the lid of the trash can closed with a metallic clang. What was that all about? Should she tell Cristina about it? After all, she and Rufino were his friends, so they were probably the best people for him to talk to. Perhaps they could make him realize that his actions weren't healthy, that refusing to discuss his loss or even look at Adriana's picture was just going to drive the pain he was suffering deeper and deeper. He would never be able to move on until he found a way of dealing with it.

On the other hand, they had probably already tried and failed. After all, Cristina had told her that Matt couldn't bear to spend time alone in his house because it was too full of memories, so she obviously knew that he wasn't coping.

Frowning, Alex turned from the trash can and placed the tray on the kitchen counter. Maybe she could help him. Sometimes it was easier to talk to a stranger, except . . . except that after spending a night in his house, she didn't feel like a stranger anymore. Nor did she think she could distance herself enough from him to be objective, even if she could persuade him to talk about Adriana, because, whether she liked it or not, she knew that she was falling for him. In fact, although she was ashamed to admit it, she even felt a tiny bit jealous of Adriana, not only because she had been so stunningly beautiful, but also because she seemed to have filled Matt's heart with so much love that he couldn't forget her; and that meant that there was no room for anyone else in his life, least of all someone as ordinary as Alex Moyer. No, she was just going to have to forget that she had ever seen the scraps of photo in the trash can.

She squared her shoulders as she turned toward the sitting room, ready to face Matt again as if nothing had happened.

By the time she limped through the doorway, however, he had gone.

Driving down the mountain road at a speed that made it seem as if he was trying to escape from something, Matt tried to calm himself. It wasn't easy. It never was when he thought of Adriana. How had he missed that photo of her, and the magazines? He thought he had cleared everything from the house. He had been so sure that there was no trace of her left, sure that he had removed her and all the memories that came with her from his life, and yet still Alex had managed to find it. She had found the torn scraps too. He had caught a glimpse of her through the half-open doorway, scraping the last of her breakfast into the trash can. Then she had leaned forward and peered into the contents before letting the lid close with a clang. After that she had just stood there, holding the tray and gazing into space.

He probably should have gone into the kitchen and given her some sort of explanation then, told her about Adriana, told her something about his life, but he hadn't been able to do it, because Alex was the last person in the world he wanted to talk to about his past. His feelings for her were already too charged with emotion to contemplate any sort of personal discussion, not if he valued his sanity. No, he had to put Alex, or at least any thought of a relationship with Alex, right out of his mind, in the same way that he had managed to banish his memories of his life with Adriana. It was the only way he could cope.

From now on he would concentrate on developing the Alcaszar and make sure that Alexandra Moyer was just another employee, someone who had come to Tenerife to do a job and who, when it was finished, would go straight back to London without making any further inroads into his heart.

Cristina, who had arrived before nine in a whirlwind of concern and fury, smiled at Alex as she sank onto the sofa.

"Matt's gone. He said he had an urgent meeting in town," she added by way of explanation.

She had regained her good humor now and was bustling around setting cushions straight and clearing away Matt's whiskey glass from the previous evening. When she had first arrived, she had been angry with both of them for not having contacted her earlier, and then she was cross with Matt for leaving Alex alone at the Alcaszar. After she had vented the worst of her tongue-lashing on him, she had turned to Alex and scolded her for wearing high heels to clamber around the overgrown garden at the hotel, ignoring Alex's protest that she had stayed on what she had thought would be a safe path. Her irritation with the pair of them finally assuaged, she had kissed them both and gone into the kitchen to make more coffee.

Alex and Matt had looked at each other and grinned. Right at that moment they had both felt like naughty children, and the conspiratorial nature of their reaction had been oddly soothing to both of them, wiping out the hidden tensions that had begun to build again as soon as Alex limped out of the bedroom into the sitting room. Swamped by a navy blue bathrobe that was at least six inches too long for her, Alex had even found herself wanting to giggle. She knew she looked ridiculous, knew the whole situation was ridiculous, and yet somehow Cristina's scolding had brought a normality that had suddenly made it easier for her to smile and joke with Matt.

That, of course, had been before she found the torn photograph. Now she wasn't sure whether she would ever be able to laugh and joke with him again.

Later, traveling back down the mountain road, Alex took the line of least resistance and agreed to visit the doctor, knowing that Cristina would not be content unless she did so. She was surprised at the affection she felt for her, considering that she had known her for such a short time. If she had thought about it, she might have recognized in her new friend her own mother's warmth and openness that, combined with a youthful vigor, made her resemble the sort of sister Alex had never had and had always wished for. She wasn't thinking of Cristina, however. All her thoughts were focused on Matt as she wondered how to best open up a discussion about his marriage to Adriana.

Finding the mutilated photograph had disturbed her more than she cared to admit. She knew his behavior wasn't the normal act of someone overcome with grief, and although she knew she was opening herself up to heartache by even thinking of him when he was so obviously unavailable, she still wanted to understand him.

"How long has Matt been on his own?" she asked at last.

Concentrating on negotiating a sharp bend in a road that had a sheer drop on one side, Cristina took a moment to answer. When she did, her reply surprised Alex.

"Nearly three years."

"Oh! I thought . . . I mean, I got the impression that it was much more recent." She paused, unsure how to take the conversation forward.

Cristina shrugged her shoulders, not taking her eyes from the road. "He had a bad time with Adriana, particularly during the final few months. I tell him he should talk about it, but he won't. He thinks he's over it, but he's not the same anymore. He's shut into himself. Before his marriage he was so lighthearted, such a funny and fun person to be with. Now . . . well, you've seen him!" She shook her head sadly as they pulled into the small parking lot at the front of the clinic.

"Was he married long?" Although Alex didn't wish to appear too inquisitive, the memory of Adriana's smiling image forced her to continue.

"Just over a year." Cristina turned off the engine and reached into the rear seat for her handbag. Then she turned and faced Alex. "Not long, but long enough to break his heart. Nothing was easy with Adriana. She was too volatile, too demanding. She wasn't really made for the everyday humdrum of marriage. Nobody that emotionally fragile is, and deep down, I think Matt knew that. That's why the end, when it came, was so painful. And of course he blamed himself, although how he thought he could have stopped her from doing what she did, I have no idea.

"Since then he has used work as a way of coping, that is, when he's not trying to shut everything that happened right out of his mind. And that's why Rufino is being so supportive about the Alcaszar, because it's the first thing that has really taken him out of himself, and when he gets excited about it, we occasionally see a glimpse of the old Matt."

She opened the driver's door, pausing as she began to climb out of the car just long enough to add, "And that's why you are so important, Alex. We need you to help make it a success. And that is why you are going to see the doctor right away, so that you can get on with your work."

She gave a sly grin, pleased that she had cleverly turned the conversation away from Matt and back to Alex's injuries.

Alex laughed, accepting that the conversation had come to an end and that she was unlikely to find out anything more about Adriana, or Matt's marriage. Frustrating as it was, she admired Cristina's loyalty. She had politely given her the bare facts without divulging any of the details of something that Matt obviously considered off-limits and not open for discussion.

As they waited for the doctor, however, Cristina's words rang in her ears. *That's why the end, when it came, was so painful. And of course he blamed himself, although how he thought he could have stopped her from doing what she did, I have no idea.*

Had Adriana committed suicide? If she had, then it was no wonder that Matt was such a screwed-up emotional mess, and it was no wonder, too, that nobody wanted to talk about it.

Chapter Eight

Cristina was in a bad mood when she returned Alex to her apartment an hour later.

"I don't understand why you must stay here when you could stay with me and I could look after you," she complained.

Alex smiled at her ill humor. "The doctor said I was fine, that I just need to rest my ankle for a week or so. He even said that I have to thank Matt for providing exactly the right treatment; so the best way that I can do that is to stay here and get on with my work. And it won't be a problem. The apartment is all on one level, so I won't have to strain my ankle; plus, I have enough food in the cupboards to last at least a week."

Although Cristina disapproved of the plan, she could see from the expression on Alex's face that she had made up her mind, so she changed tack. "In that case I will visit you every day so that I can check on your recovery and make sure that you are eating properly."

"You're a dear!" Alex told her, leaning heavily on her arm as she carefully inched her way down the path to the front door. "And I shall look forward to your visits."

As they reached the front door, they turned and gave each other a smile of mutual respect, both of them recognizing that they had met their match, and it was this that began to cement their friendship into something that would become more and more important to Alex over the coming months.

Once Cristina had established that everything Alex needed was within reach, she made her a mug of coffee, left a tuna salad covered in plastic wrap in the refrigerator, and then, promising to return later in the day, went home to where her mother was yet again caring for her small sons.

Left to her own devices, Alex limped out onto the balcony and sat in a comfortable rattan chair for the time it took to finish her coffee. The sun was already hot, so she was delighted when she saw that there was a canvas awning rolled up above the patio door. At least that would allow her to spend some of her time working in the fresh air once she had organized herself.

She went back inside the apartment and rinsed her mug at the sink. Then, propping herself up on a tall stool, she called the office from the telephone on the kitchen counter. Conchita answered.

"Alex!" The warm relief in her strongly accented voice was both unexpected and welcome. "I'm so glad you're okay. Matt told me about your accident. Have you seen a doctor?"

"Yes, and he says I'm fine. I just feel . . . well, I feel a bit ticked off actually," Alex said with a sigh. "Nobody has given me any credit for sticking to the path and trying to be careful. You would think I dug that hole under the flagstone myself, the amount of grief everyone has given me. Even the doctor was cross with me for wearing what he called ridiculous shoes."

Conchita gave a warm chuckle full of real amusement. "Ah, but he is not a woman. I understand completely. I too am . . . how do you say it . . . challenged with the height!"

Alex gave an answering laugh. "Oh, that's such music to my ears! After so much scolding from everyone else, it's so good to have just one person on my side."

They exchanged a few more pleasantries until, learning that Alex would be working from home until her ankle was strong enough to manage the challenge of the steep hill into town and the steps into the office building, Conchita quickly moved into administrative mode. Her practical suggestions impressed Alex, and before long they had compiled a list of everything she needed to start on the first phase of her designs.

"I'll deliver everything at lunchtime," Conchita told her.

"Rufino is in the office all day, so he can answer the telephone."

Alex thanked her and hung up. She was amused at the cavalier way Conchita organized both her employers. Strong and opinionated women seemed to be the norm in Tenerife, or maybe it was just Conchita and Cristina.

When Conchita arrived, she brought lunch as well as several boxes containing all the items that Alex would need to work from home. She dumped everything onto the kitchen counter and looked around the apartment approvingly.

"This is a good work environment," she said. "Cool, uncluttered, lots of space."

"It is," Alex agreed. "But it will be better if we rearrange some of the furniture. I did try, but I couldn't manage," she added apologetically.

"I should think not." Conchita gave her the same fierce sort of look she had already received from Cristina several times that morning. "I will do it. Just tell me where."

Between them they managed to shift the furniture so that the table was within easy reach of the telephone and the plug sockets that she would need for a computer. Then Conchita stacked the boxes of stationery on the floor against the wall, well away from anywhere that Alex might walk, and she moved the armchair so that it no longer impeded the door to the balcony. After that she tackled the balcony itself, pulling the patio table and two upright chairs well away from the door before stacking the rest in a corner. She left the comfortable rattan recliner at the edge of the balcony so that Alex could sit in the sun and enjoy the view.

"Now there is no excuse for a further accident," she said sternly, brushing a powdering of dust from her navy skirt.

"Are you Cristina's sister?" Alex blurted out, struck once again by a resemblance in manner, although, apart from their dark hair, there was little physical likeness. Conchita was shorter and thinner, with sharper features, and her straight hair was cut into a spiky urchin crop.

She roared with laughter at Alex's question. "No! I'm just her friend. We've known each other since we were tiny babies, though. We went to school together, and to college, and even went on our first date together, so I guess the same things have influenced us."

Thinking how comfortable it must be to have such a friend, to be able to share the joys and despairs of life from childhood to adulthood without explanation or excuse, Alex pushed away a feeling of envy. Moving to London to study and work, and then meeting Rory and fitting in with the demands of his life, meant that she had more or less lost touch with all her old friends. Only Bethany remained, and even she was a friend from college. Alex couldn't think of a single soul other than her parents, brother, and a solitary aunt whom she still knew from her childhood.

"You're so lucky to live here," she said as Conchita unwrapped sandwiches and poured juice into two glasses. "The weather is wonderful, of course, but I don't just mean that. I love the fact that everyone seems to know one another. It's a real community. That's something that doesn't happen in a big city."

"You're only looking at the surface," Conchita replied, carrying their lunch out to the balcony. "In a small town like this everyone knows your business, and that can be very difficult to cope with. Ask Matt!"

She was too busy fixing a pole to the canvas awning so that she could pull it out to immediately see the expression of inquiry on Alex's face, and when she did notice it, the telephone was ringing. It was Rufino, needing some information for a client. First he spoke to Alex, wanting to know how she was, and then he had a long and involved conversation with Conchita. Finally she slammed down the telephone with a huge sigh.

"We don't employ enough staff," she said. "I keep telling Matt and Rufino that one day everything will come crashing about their ears, but they just laugh at me. When you are well enough to come into the office, Alex, you'll see what I mean."

And that, thought Alex half an hour later as she watched

Conchita drive away, *is all I'm going to get. Whatever happened in Matt's life, I'm not going to know about the details, because all his friends are determined to protect him.*

Alex's life over the next few days developed into a regular pattern. After an early breakfast she would answer phone calls from Cristina and from Conchita and assure them both that she was well, had slept well, and that her ankle was recovering. Then she would work steadily until lunchtime, when Conchita would arrive with any necessary supplies, as well as a sandwich or an enchilada, juice, or, occasionally, an icy bottle of lager.

After a pleasant thirty-minute break, when they talked about everything under the sun except Matt, she would resume working until about four, when Cristina would arrive, sometimes alone but usually with the twins.

Soon Alex found herself glancing at the clock at regular intervals during the afternoon, hoping, as it crept toward four o'clock, that this would be another day when Luis and Nicolas would accompany their mother. She loved to see them. They were interested in everything and inspected her books, the kitchen cupboards, the things on her dressing table, even her handbag, and yet they never broke anything. They would pick something up and bring it to her, their eyes bright with intelligence as they waited for her to tell them what it was in English.

At first Cristina had tried to control them, fussing every time they touched anything other than the toys she had brought with her; but when she realized that Alex didn't mind, she began to relax and join in by providing the Spanish word for each item.

Soon the twins began to mix English words with their native Spanish when they spoke to Alex, and she, in turn, found her rusty, schoolgirl Spanish coming back to her, so that when, one day, they produced a simple storybook from their bag of toys, she realized she could read it. Delighted, they insisted on sitting one on each knee as she stumbled through the pronunciation, and then clapped excitedly when she finished.

She met Cristina's eyes with a self-conscious smile. "That

feels like a bigger achievement than anything else I've done this week," she said.

"You're a natural," Cristina told her. "Would you like children of your own one day?"

"More than anything, but that's not so easy without a prospective father on the scene." Alex deflected the sudden clutch at her heart with dismissive humor. What if she never managed to have children? She was already twenty-seven, and with no sign of anyone on the horizon who wanted the sort of family life she aspired to, here she was settling for the sort of promise she had glimpsed in Francesco Pascual's eyes. She shrugged away the feeling of loneliness such thoughts engendered and changed the subject.

Chapter Nine

On the sixth day of Alex's forced incarceration, Conchita arrived as usual, except that this time she was hidden behind an enormous bouquet of flowers. A surprised Alex took it from her, wondering, for one heart-stopping moment, if it was from Matt. She had tried not to mind the fact that he hadn't once telephoned to see how she was. Common sense told her that he was busy and that, anyway, Conchita would keep him up to date with her progress, so she was surprised at how disappointed she felt when she saw that the flowers were from Francesco Pascual. The writing on the accompanying card was black and bold and full of flattery as well as good wishes for a speedy recovery. He had printed his phone number under a flamboyant signature.

"He came to the office to invite you to lunch," Conchita explained with a twinkle in her eye. "So naturally I was forced to tell him about your injuries, and within two hours he had delivered this to your desk with strict instructions that it should be conveyed to you immediately! I'm not sure whether to be more impressed by your ability to attract members of the opposite sex despite being out of action, or by the sensitivity of Francesco's antennae toward someone new in town!"

Alex, chiding herself for her ungrateful sense of disappointment, grinned at Conchita. "We quite literally bumped into each other on my first day, and he seemed . . . interested!"

"To put it mildly, I'd say! You need to watch him, though. He is a real ladies' man, although he can be great fun if you don't mind your men shallow and self-obsessed. He'll give

72

you a really good time while you're in Tenerife, but he's definitely not someone for the long haul."

"Then he will suit me just fine, because right at this moment I am very decidedly a short-haul sort of girl!"

They both burst into laughter at Alex's flippant remark, and then, while she found a vase and arranged the flowers, and Conchita organized lunch, they continued to discuss Francesco's reputation and character. To Alex he sounded harmless. In fact he sounded much like Rory, always focused on having a good time, attending the best party, enjoying a good restaurant. Well, she could do worse. At least nothing about him would surprise her, and she would get to see the island as well. Her problem with Rory had been the fact that she had given him her heart, and she certainly didn't intend to do that with Francesco Pascual.

She didn't telephone Francesco to thank him for the flowers until the next day, partly because she was busy and partly because she was determined to keep their relationship casual in the extreme. When she did telephone, however, his apparent pleasure at hearing her voice was both flattering and seductive. They exchanged pleasantries for several minutes, and then he invited her out to lunch the following day, promising that he wouldn't take her anywhere that involved steps.

For a moment she hesitated, but then she thought of the long hours she had put into her designs each evening, as well as during the weekend, and decided that she deserved some time off. When she agreed, he wrote down her address and said he would collect her at twelve thirty.

Conchita, on learning that she was to be relegated to second-class lunch companion on the following day, pretended chagrin until her dimples showed through. "I guess you have to repay him for those wonderful flowers." She sighed. "What would I give to have someone like Francesco fall at my feet for just a little while?"

Alex dressed with more care than usual the following morning, hiding her bandaged ankle under silk trousers with a matching top, and slipping her feet into a pair of flat, beaded sandals. Surveying her image in the full-length mirror in the bedroom, she decided to sweep her hair up onto the top of her head to give herself some height. When she had finished, she added a hibiscus flower from the bush outside the front door and then, satisfied with the end result, returned to her work while she waited for Francesco.

He arrived promptly and was solicitous in both manner and actions, asking her how she was, helping her in and out of his car, pulling out her chair at the restaurant, all of which he managed to do while quite blatantly flirting with her. She laughed at him, refusing to take him seriously, and concentrated on the menu.

Over *pollo conajo,* which turned out to be chicken fillet in a garlic sauce, served with crusty bread and fresh green vegetables, Alex and Francesco began to get to know each other. She learned that he, too, worked in the property market like Matt but that he concentrated on rentals and sales rather than development.

"It gives me more time to enjoy myself," he told her. "I could not, like some, spend all my time working. There is too much pleasure to be had in life for me to want to shut myself up in an office all day making money."

While part of Alex agreed with him, she wasn't about to say so when his remarks were so obviously aimed at Matt. Instead, she lifted her glass of crisp, dry white wine.

"Here's to pleasure, then," she said, giving him a level look over the rim of the glass.

Francesco raised his own glass to his lips with a wicked grin. "Much pleasure indeed," he murmured.

As they toasted each other, the waiter showed two people to the table next to them. One of them was Matt, and he gave her a cool nod as he pulled out a chair in her direct line of vision. Then he ignored her, concentrating instead on his companion, a plump, middle-aged man who kept mopping at his forehead with a white handkerchief as he studied the menu.

For Alex the rest of the meal was spoiled. Although Francesco tempted her to order a delicious-looking dessert, it tasted like sawdust when she ate it. She refused coffee, pleading too much work as a poor excuse.

When they finally got up to leave, she stuck out her chin in a way that would have filled those who knew her well with foreboding. Whatever his personal hang-ups, how dare Matt treat her in such a dismissive manner! She worked for him, for goodness' sake. She had even slept at his house, borrowed his robe, shared the sort of intimacies usually reserved for close friends, and yet he was totally ignoring her. Apart from that first cool greeting, he was behaving as if she didn't exist. Not once had she seen him look at her, although, against her will, her own eyes had frequently strayed in his direction.

She allowed Francesco to take her arm but refused to move past Matt's table. He glanced up and then immediately rose to his feet, but not before she had seen a look of intense irritation shadow his face. When he spoke to her, however, his voice gave little away.

"Alex, I'm glad to see that your ankle is almost better."

She gave an impatient little shrug, because she wasn't there to pass the time of day. "I still can't manage stairs, I'm afraid, but I'm sure I'll be fine in a few more days."

"In that case, we'll look forward to having you back in the office soon."

Really, he was the most aggravating man. Was he deliberately trying to rile her with his disinterested formality, or was he really not aware of how rude he was being? He made no attempt to introduce her to his lunch companion, and he only acknowledged Francesco with the slightest of nods. She gritted her teeth.

"I need a meeting with you and Rufino," she blurted out, knowing, as she did so, that she was being childish. What was wrong with telephoning him at the office to discuss it? Why had she chosen to do it in the middle of a restaurant and in the middle of what was probably a business lunch? Because she was angry, that was why! Angry at the way he had washed his hands of her as soon as Cristina had arrived at his house. Angry at the way he was behaving now, as if she were a child who needed humoring rather than someone who was supposedly here to help make his fortune.

"I'll get Conchita to ring you to schedule a time in the calendar" was all he said, and then he more or less dismissed her by bowing his head slightly and moving his chair.

"Fine." She gave his startled companion the widest smile she could summon and then limped toward the door as fast as her still-painful ankle would allow.

Francesco slipped an arm around her shoulders in an attempt to slow her down. "He is not worth getting angry about, Alexandra. He has no manners. Forget him, and think about this evening, when I am going to take you to listen to some of the best music in Tenerife."

She gave him an automatic smile, barely noticing that he had already assumed ownership of her social life. She was still thinking about Matt and wondering if Francesco was right and that he wasn't worth getting angry about, when she met the full force of his gaze through the window as she limped past the restaurant toward Francesco's car. She felt herself recoil a little. Why had she ever thought that his eyes were blue? From where she was looking they were a bleak, bleak gray and as cold as the sea in winter.

She found it difficult to concentrate on her work for the rest of the afternoon; not that it really mattered, because she had already completed as much as she could without either returning to the Alcaszar or spending some time with Matt and Rufino.

Even Cristina's visit failed to lift her, and she was glad, for once, that Luis and Nicolas had elected to stay with their grandmother.

"You look tired," Cristina accused her. "Is your ankle troubling you?"

"No, it's fine," Alex reassured her. "I've just been working late, trying to get everything done as soon as possible."

"Then it's time you had a change of scenery. Why don't you

come home with me and spend the evening with us? The twins will be so excited."

"I'd love to, but I can't." Alex's regret was genuine. "I've already agreed to go out with Francesco. He's taking me to listen to some live music."

"Then you will be even more tired tomorrow," Cristina scolded. "Let this be your first lesson on our local nightlife. Nothing on the island starts until very late." Then she laughed. "Don't mind me. I'm just a jealous old married woman. You go and enjoy yourself, but close your eyes on the mountain roads, because Francesco drives like the very devil."

Several hours later, closely confined in Francesco's bright red, low-slung coupe, Alex discovered just what Cristina meant. With the windows open and music blaring from stereo speakers, he zigzagged down the mountain roads at top speed, using his horn at every corner and laughing triumphantly each time he managed to overtake another driver on the narrow road. By the time they were cruising along the wide boulevards of the busy coastal area, she was a nervous wreck. Far from being closed as Cristina had suggested, her eyes had been out on stalks for the entire journey as she wondered if she and Francesco would make it safely to their destination.

"Too fast?" he asked her, noticing her tense expression for the first time as he parked the car.

"Too fast!" she agreed firmly. "If you want me to come out with you again, Francesco, then we'll have to reach an agreement about your driving."

He grinned at her. "With me you will have to learn to live a little. This is not London with its stop-start traffic and its congestion zones. This is Tenerife!"

She frowned. "You make it sound like a challenge."

"Maybe that's what it is." He unfastened his seat belt and swung his long legs out of the car.

Waiting for him to open her door and help her out, Alex considered his words. Was she up to the sort of challenge he was talking about? Was she ready to throw caution to the wind and pretend she was seventeen again, or was she going to turn her back on an opportunity to have a bit of fun for the first time in ages just because Francesco was reckless?

Later, sitting at the dimly lit bar of a rustic nightclub and listening to a very talented jazz singer, she admitted to herself that she was having a good time. Francesco had introduced her to a number of his friends, who, although the music made it difficult to talk, all seemed very pleasant. Admittedly some of the women were a lot younger and prone to giggling and going to the bathroom in pairs, but they smiled at Alex when she looked at them, and two of them openly admired her dress.

She had chosen a full-length slinky black halter dress, with a pattern of sequins stitched around the neckline, and teamed it with a pair of low-heeled black sandals. Although they weren't ideal, they barely showed beneath the dress, and with her hair still piled high on top of her head, she knew she looked good. And the expression in Francesco's eyes whenever he spoke to her made it clear he thought she did too.

She sat back, letting the velvety sound of the music wash over her. After so long, it felt good to be out socializing again, and to be with someone who obviously found her attractive. She turned to ask Francesco a question about the singer, but he was in the middle of a spirited conversation with two of his friends, so instead she gazed idly around the room. There were one or two tourists propping up the bar, but the majority of people appeared to be Spanish. This was obviously a place mostly patronized by islanders. Her gaze wandered on, taking in the singer, his musicians, and the true music aficionados who were sitting as close to him as possible and listening with a breathless attention, until finally it rested on a group near the door; or, more particularly, on one person in the group by the door. Matt!

She caught her breath as a surge of emotion shifted deep inside her at the sudden and unexpected sight of him. Determinedly, she pushed the feeling away. He *would* appear just when she was beginning to enjoy herself! Was he following her or something? Well, this time he could have a taste of his own medicine. She gave him a cool nod as their eyes met, and then she looked away. When, much later, and unable to help herself, her gaze circled the room again, someone else was sitting in his seat. He had gone.

Chapter Ten

Alex was still in her robe when Conchita telephoned early the next morning to tell her that Matt and Rufino were both free at eleven o'clock and would come to meet with her. She gave an inward groan as they scheduled a meeting. Although she wasn't going to admit it to Conchita, she was very definitely the worse for wear this morning, the result of foolishly drinking coffee far too late in the evening and then not getting enough sleep. She glanced at the clock above the kitchen counter. Ten o'clock. That didn't give her much time to get ready.

She hurried into the shower and, in an attempt to wake herself up, let the water splash over her until it began to run cold. Then she pulled on a pair of jeans and a white T-shirt and twisted her wet hair into a tight topknot. A quick glance in the mirror assured her that, despite her late night, she didn't look too bad. Eating and working outside over the past week had tanned her skin to a smooth golden brown, so she needed only a dab of blusher and a slick of lip gloss to look presentable.

Food! She limped back into the open-plan kitchen. She must have some food or she wouldn't be able to concentrate on the forthcoming meeting. She gulped down a glass of orange juice and then hurriedly poured cereal and milk into a bowl, topped it with a large dollop of yogurt, and ate standing up. She had only just finished when the doorbell rang. Cursing under her breath, she opened the door.

Matt stood outside holding a laptop computer under one arm and a printer under the other. "I hope I'm not too early," he said. "Conchita has been asking me to set this up for you for days."

Alex stood back wordlessly so that he could carry the equipment through. Then, as she closed the door behind him, she had a sudden recollection of the pristine tidiness of his apartment, and she found herself wanting to push ahead of him so that she could close the bedroom door before he saw the disarray of her unmade bed and the pile of clothes she had thrown across a chair the previous evening.

Matt, however, walked straight ahead without glancing left or right. When he reached the main room, he lowered the computer and printer onto the table and flexed his arms. Then he looked around for a plug. Finding one next to the telephone socket, he began to busy himself with setting everything up on the dining room table.

Alex retreated to the kitchen area, where she hastily rinsed her breakfast things and returned the milk and yogurt to the refrigerator. She still hadn't spoken when Matt, without turning around, asked her to find a double-sided plug in the rucksack he had slung onto the floor.

She did as he asked; then she picked up a large blue folder from the kitchen counter, intending to calm her frazzled nerves by sorting her designs into a logical sequence in preparation for their meeting.

She had only flicked through half a dozen when Matt spoke again. "Did you enjoy the music last night?" he asked, his voice sounding very matter-of-fact, which, given his usual attitude when he saw her with Francesco, surprised her.

"Yes, I did. I had an altogether pleasant evening." Alex couldn't see his reaction, because he was detangling wires under the table.

He didn't reply until he had crawled out from under the table and was standing upright again. Then he looked at her and, to her astonishment, gave what could almost be classified as a friendly smile.

"Good. I'm glad you're beginning to enjoy Tenerife after

such a difficult start. You'll find there are lots of places that offer live music and dancing, although not many offer anything as good as last night's singer. I try to catch at least one of his performances whenever he visits Tenerife."

Rendered almost speechless by his unexpectedly friendly manner, Alex gave a weak nod as she offered coffee.

Murmuring his thanks, Matt disappeared beneath the table again. Left with his back view for a second time, Alex, totally thrown by his attitude after the previous day's cold shoulder, made a face at him. Then she filled the kettle with water and spooned coffee into a cafetiere that she had found at the back of one of the kitchen cupboards. By the time the kettle had boiled and she had put mugs, milk, and sugar onto a tray, Matt had finished and Rufino had arrived. All three of them went out onto the balcony and looked at the view.

"Cristina says that you like it here." Rufino accepted his coffee with a smile of thanks.

"I do! The view is simply spectacular, and the apartment is so light and spacious compared to my apartment in London. Goodness knows how I will readjust when I return home."

They continued to chat politely for the few minutes it took them to finish their coffee, and then, feeling distinctly nervous, Alex led them back inside and began to present her hand-drawn visuals by laying them down, one by one, on the dining room table. She had used ink and color wash to sketch her designs onto the left-hand side of the page and had listed the details in clear print on the right.

"I started at the top of the hotel," she explained. "Because there are no structural alterations involved, I knew that designing the bedroom suites would be relatively easy. All I needed was to come up with an appropriately coordinated color scheme that could be adapted from room to room and floor to floor. You can see how each design flows into the next one, while this page is a universal plan for the corridors. And these are separate plans for each of the public elevator areas, because I think each one should have an identifying signature, such as a painting or a sculpture—something that will help the guests recognize it as 'their floor.' "

Matt and Rufino carefully studied every detail, occasionally nodding or flicking back through the pages to check something. When she felt she had given them enough time to at least get a feel for her suggestions, she produced another set of designs, this time for the ground floor.

"These are far less detailed because I need to spend more time studying the shape of the rooms and the way the light falls, but as these show, my initial visit did give me some ideas, and I would really appreciate your comments before I go again."

On tenterhooks now, she looked at their faces. Rufino, to her great relief, was smiling approvingly, but as usual, Matt was giving nothing away. She found herself panicking. Perhaps he didn't like her designs. Although they had discussed a few possibilities while she was lying on the sofa in his house, they hadn't had time to flesh out those ideas, so Alex just hoped that her interpretation was close to what he wanted. She looked at him again. His face was so expressionless that she wanted to slap some enthusiasm into it.

"Perhaps you would prefer to talk in private," she blurted out, her anxiety making her unable to stay silent for a moment longer. "I mean, you might need time to think about my ideas and then get back to me."

The two men looked at each other, and then Matt shook his head. "I don't think so, but thanks anyway. You seem to have really grasped what we want, and I, for one, am more than happy to go with your suggestions."

"You really mean that?" Suddenly Alex found that she couldn't stop smiling, as excitement bubbled up inside her at the thought of putting her hard work into practice. It was always the same when she designed something: hours and hours of thinking and slogging over pages and pages of paper and then, at the end of it, if she had done her job well, the opportunity to realize her ideas, make them more than outline sketches filled with color wash. Make them real.

Unable to help himself, Matt grinned at her. He didn't want to get too excited in case it all went wrong, but her enthusiasm was so contagious that he could almost believe that the Alcaszar would soon be more than an empty shell with peeling paint and out-of-date décor. Thanks to Alex's inspiration, it was halfway to becoming what he had always dreamed of, a hotel to be reckoned with.

Rufino smiled when he saw Matt's elation. "This calls for a celebration," he said. "I'll phone Conchita and ask her to join us with some food and beer."

After a short but very jolly lunch, during which they all tried to come up with names for the various suites and public rooms at the Alcaszar with very little success, Conchita and Rufino left for separate appointments. Matt, however, stayed to check that the computer and printer would do all that Alex required of them.

While she stacked the lunch plates and glasses in the sink, he cleared her visuals from the table and slid them back into their folder. Then he moved a second chair close to the computer and waited for her to join him.

Unexpectedly unnerved by his proximity, she was all fingers and thumbs when she first used the keyboard, but as soon as her design program loaded, she forgot that it was Matt who was sitting with her and just treated him like any other client, explaining that she would scan the hand-drawn visuals into the machine and then begin to translate them into the more detailed portfolio that she needed to get things moving.

Matt tried hard to concentrate on what she was saying. He was certainly impressed by what she had done so far. In fact, he was far more impressed than he had expected to be. Having seen her laughing and drinking with Francesco Pascual twice in the past twenty-four hours, he hadn't really believed that she would have put in the necessary slog to complete such a large amount of work in so short a time. Now he felt ashamed of himself for having had such ungenerous thoughts. Her drawings, her logical thinking, and her enthusiastic presentation this morning had all shown her to be the dedicated and professional designer Tom Curzon had told him to expect. He pulled his thoughts back to the here and now as she turned to him.

"Do you want me to source the decorating materials and other stuff?" she asked. "Or should I work from a list of your suppliers?"

Matt couldn't tear his eyes away from her gaze. He was mesmerized by it. He noticed that her eyes had tiny flecks of gold that reflected the sunlight streaming in through the window. He wanted to count the freckles that had multiplied across her nose in the sun, he wanted to slide his arm around her shoulders and pull her close. He wanted to kiss her!

Hurriedly squashing his thoughts, he pulled himself together and straightened up, agreeing that a coordinated effort would be best if they were to source everything they needed in the shortest possible time.

"I'll ask Conchita to send you a list of our suppliers now that you have e-mail," he said, clearing the huskiness from his voice. "That way you can look them up on the Internet as well as contact them directly. If you need any help, just call me. Daytime or evenings are all the same to me, so anytime is fine."

Alex nodded and turned back to the computer screen, not because she needed to but because she wanted something to distract her from that sudden flare of interest she had seen in Matt's eyes. She was totally confused by him. Why did he have such mood swings? Was it the result of his loneliness, or the traumatic end to his marriage, or was it something to do with her? Sometimes, like just a moment ago, she was sure that he found her as attractive as she found him.

She felt him shift in the seat beside her and knew that he was preparing to leave. Suddenly she didn't want him to. She wanted to spend more time with him. In spite of herself, she wanted another chance to learn more about him.

"I'm thirsty," she murmured, and pushing back her own chair, she limped across to the kitchen area. "Would you like a drink? Juice, a beer, coffee?" She opened the fridge as she spoke and pulled out a can of cola.

She sensed his hesitation, but then he nodded. "Thanks, I'll have one of those."

Handing him a can, she moved across to the balcony and fitted a pole to the canopy so that she could pull it down to shade them from the fierce afternoon sun. Matt was there before her, taking it out of her hand and yanking the canopy out to its full extent. Then he moved her rattan recliner into the shade before sitting opposite her, astride the upright chair that she used when she was working.

Unwilling to engage in any personal conversation that might close him up again, Alex continued to talk about the Alcaszar. "It's such a muddle of poor design." She sighed.

"I take it you don't approve of the original heavy Victorian furniture, then?" Matt teased.

He was so genuinely amused by her disgust that he forgot himself, forgot his intention to keep his distance and became, for the first time since they'd met, the real Matt, the one Cristina had told her about.

"I certainly don't." Alex returned his smile. "I've studied the old photos, and how anyone could ever have thought that such a sunny climate was the right place for thick carpets, flocked wallpaper, and heavy drapes beats me! The whole place cries out for pale colors and for natural wood and stone."

"You'd be surprised how well the contents sale went when the original owners sold out," he told her. "It seems that everyone in town had room for one piece of Victoriana."

"But surely that was before your time?" Alex was surprised, because she knew that the Alcaszar had been closed for at least twenty years. Matt shook his head.

"It was while I was at school, but I still remember it. I spent hours wandering around the hotel looking at the different lots. I think that was when I first decided I wanted it, even though I was little more than a child at the time."

"But surely . . . I mean you weren't born here, were you? I thought Tom said he met you in London."

Alex's interested inquiry broke through Matt's final reserve, and before he realized what he was doing, he started to talk about his past. "He did, but we met while I was studying. Before that I lived on Tenerife. My parents moved here when I was about ten, to manage a hotel, believe it or not. I kicked up such a fuss when they tried to leave me behind at boarding school that in the end they brought me with them and sent me to the local school, where I learned fluent Spanish and graduated with honors in fishing, surfing, and the jazz trombone."

He chuckled at the expression on her face. "It took me a long time to realize that I needed some serious qualifications if I was going to make a living for myself. Eventually I went back to England and trained as a surveyor, and that's when I met Tom Curzon."

"And then you went into partnership with Rufino."

"Not straightaway. I worked in London for several years. In fact, Tom and I shared an apartment there and lived it up pretty well every night. It was only when he married Elspeth that I decided to come back to Tenerife for a year or two. Fortunately for me, the first person I met up with when I returned was Rufino, who was an old friend. The rest, as they say, is history."

"Do your parents still live here?" Alex asked, feeling that she was getting somewhere at last and wondering whether she would have enough nerve to lead the conversation around to his marriage.

"They do." He nodded. "Like me, they can't do without the sun for long, although now that they've retired, they're often away traveling, or visiting the UK to see my sisters and their children. What about your parents?"

"Oh, they're mostly on vacation these days, either visiting my brother in New Zealand or joining up with friends for walking tours or some winter sunshine. I don't get to see them as much as I should," she admitted.

"Will they come out to visit you while you're here?"

Alex shook her head a little wistfully. "I don't think so. They know I'm busy. I'll make sure I spend some time with them when I go home, though."

"That's a shame, because Tenerife is a great place for a vacation. You mustn't work so hard that you miss out on sightseeing while you're here. Maybe I could show you around a bit on Saturday."

Where had that come from? What had prompted him to ask her to join him when all his senses had told him to keep his distance? He met her startled gaze head-on. Well, he certainly deserved that. After all, he hadn't exactly covered himself in glory as far as his recent behavior toward her was concerned, had he? He could hardly blame her if she turned him down. She didn't, though.

"I'd . . . I'd love that," she said.

The shadow of the canopy hid the flush that suffused her cheeks as she answered him. Did he really want to take her out, or was he just being polite? Then she remembered the look in his eyes when they had sat close together in front of the computer, and she knew that there was more to it than that. Despite the emotional mess that Adriana had left behind, he was interested in her—she was sure of it. A feeling of anticipation surged through her. Then she remembered that she had already agreed to go out with Francesco on Saturday, and her heart sank. At the same moment, the telephone rang.

As she went to answer it, she heard Matt's chair scrape against the tiles, and by the time she lifted the receiver, he had retrieved his rucksack from beneath the table and was stuffing superfluous computer wires and connectors back into it.

"Hello, beautiful Alexandra." Much to her chagrin, the receiver was on speakerphone, so although Francesco's voice was low and deliberately seductive, it still echoed loudly around the room. "Are you ready for another night of excitement with me?"

As their "night of excitement" had ended with a chaste kiss on the cheek as Francesco dropped her on her doorstep at two in the morning, Alex laughed.

"Hello, Francesco. I'm a working girl, so I'm not up for too much excitement in one week."

"Pah! You know what I say about too much work. It kills the soul!"

Alex's amused smile died as she saw Matt make his way toward the door. Surely he wasn't going, not now when they needed to talk, to make arrangements. And surely he couldn't believe that anyone as obvious as Francesco really interested her.

"I'm calling to check that you're still okay for Saturday," Francesco persisted. "You did say that you'd like to hear some more live music, so I've thought of a new and much more exciting place to take you."

The sight of Matt's disappearing back distracted Alex. When he reached the door, he turned around and lifted his hand in a brief salute of farewell. Then he was gone.

Upset by his abrupt departure, she didn't have the patience to flirt with Francesco. After agreeing to meet at eight, she cut him short on the pretext that she was busy and returned the telephone to its cradle.

Matt, meanwhile, was furious with himself. What had he been thinking to open up to Alex like that, to say nothing about inviting her out? Admittedly their conversation had been harmless, just the sort of casual socializing that might take place in any bar or restaurant on Tenerife between people who hadn't known each other for very long. If Francesco hadn't telephoned, however, there was no knowing what else he might have shared with her. Seduced by her interest, he had come close to disclosing more of his past, as well as the story behind the acquisition of the Alcaszar, and that was something he couldn't afford to do while she was seeing Francesco Pascual.

He walked swiftly back to the office with a frown on his face. He wished that Tom Curzon had sent anyone but Alex. It didn't matter that she was possibly one of the best designers he'd worked with in a long while, such was her instinctive grasp of his project. Her presence on the island was complicating everything, and now, despite his determination to keep her out of his life, he had offered to show her the island. Thank goodness Francesco had telephoned in time to bring him to his senses, because he certainly wasn't prepared to share Alex with *him*. If she was still dating Francesco, then he was going to forget that he had ever invited her out and leave her to her own devices.

Conchita, catching a glimpse of Matt's face as he strode past her into his office, kept her head down. What had happened now? she wondered. Surely he hadn't fallen out with Alex, although in his present mood she knew that he was quite capable of falling out with anyone. Was it something to do with the Alcaszar yet again? Although she was as excited as the rest of them about the prospect of turning it into the tasteful and secluded retreat that Matt envisioned, she was getting just a bit fed up with the way it was taking over everything else. Anyone would think that they didn't have other work piling up, the same as anyone who didn't know him like she did would think that he wasn't interested in Alex.

Conchita, however, had been at the receiving end of his constant inquiries about Alex's injuries since her accident at the hotel. She had also noticed his irritation every time Francesco Pascual's name was mentioned, and she had seen the grim frown on his face when that huge bouquet of flowers was delivered to Alex's desk. She decided that as soon as she had the chance, she would talk to Cristina about it.

Chapter Eleven

For the next few days Alex reverted to working long hours. Once she had scanned in her hand-drawn visuals, she concentrated on tidying them up. When she was satisfied, she started to develop some of her other ideas. She also started to contact Matt's suppliers to arrange appointments for the following week, when she was sure that her ankle would be sufficiently strong for her to return to the office.

Overall she was pleased with how things were going. Although she was used to working on deadline, she couldn't remember another project where her ideas had flowed so smoothly. She was eager now to return to the Alcaszar and irritated that she couldn't yet because of her damaged ankle. She was determined to buy herself some sneakers. Those and a pair of flat, sturdy sandals would be far more sensible than the high heels she normally wore, except in the evenings, of course.

The thought prompted an image of Francesco, and she sighed. He telephoned her every day, sometimes twice a day, and while it was pleasant to be admired, she wasn't altogether happy with the way their conversations were going. For a start, his flirting was becoming boring. She was too sophisticated to be taken in by the seductive murmurings that he had obviously found successful with younger and less experienced girls. Increasingly, too, he kept asking her about the Alcaszar and showing a great interest in her designs, which she should have found flattering but which, for reasons that she couldn't fathom, she didn't.

In spite of her misgivings, however, she had continued to

91

meet him after work, partly because she was fed up with her own company despite Cristina and Conchita's frequent visits, and partly to keep her mind off Matt. She had not seen him again since his abrupt departure, nor had she spoken to him. All her telephone conversations were with Conchita, who faithfully conveyed messages to Matt and vice versa, as required.

Now, when she met Francesco, however, she insisted, despite his protestations, on sharing the cost of their meals. There was no way that she was going to let him think that he could buy her affections. A kiss on the cheek or her hand on his arm was all that she was prepared to offer.

When Saturday night arrived, Alex was feeling more her old self. For a start, her ankle was so much better that she had taken a gentle walk into town that morning to buy the sensible sneakers she had promised herself. To her delight the shop had had several pairs in her size, all in bright, edgy colors. Determined to be as fashionable as possible even with flat, functional shoes, she had bought two pairs, one in scarlet and the other in a more muted blue. She had also bought a pair of sensible walking sandals, as well as some flip-flops that sported a bright assortment of colored beads. Pleased with her purchases, she had then booked a rental car for the following week so that she could visit some of Matt's suppliers as well as spend more time at the Alcaszar without having to rely on anyone else.

Conchita had promised to sort out transportation for her as and when she needed it, but Alex didn't want to be reliant on anyone, least of all Matt. Nor did she wish to limit her leisure time to the sort of hair-raising journeys that Francesco provided. She wanted to enjoy her time on Tenerife as much as possible, and that meant being free to explore the island at leisure and, if she so chose, alone.

She had spent the rest of the afternoon sunbathing on her balcony, determined to rest her ankle enough for it to cope with a couple of dances during the evening.

Francesco had suggested they go to a popular venue in the

main tourist center of Playa de las Americas. He had told her that it was well known for its good food, spectacular cabaret, and also for its outdoor dancing. As her evening wasn't starting until eight o'clock, Alex decided to have a leisurely bath instead of her usual quick shower, and to take her time getting ready.

She had just thrown her clothes into the laundry basket and turned off the bath tap when someone rang the bell. With an exclamation of annoyance, she wrapped herself in a large towel and made her way to the door. It was Matt!

She stared at him in disbelief. He certainly had a way of turning up at the oddest moments. Not a telephone call or a visit all week, yet now he was standing on her doorstep at six o'clock on a Saturday night holding what looked like a box of vegetables. He was dressed in the sort of smart, casual clothes that indicated he was on his way to somewhere special.

He nodded at the towel. "Sorry! I've obviously caught you at a bad time."

"I was just about to take a bath," she told him a little frostily, clutching the towel more tightly as the long, lean sight of him propped nonchalantly against the door frame began to stir unwanted flutterings in her stomach.

"Cristina asked me to drop these off. They're from her mother's garden," he explained. "Although if I'd realized you were going out, I would have delivered them tomorrow morning."

Alex was nonplussed. She had already arranged to see Cristina and Rufino the following day, so she couldn't understand why the vegetables couldn't have waited twenty-four hours.

"Are you going somewhere nice?" Matt appeared to be oblivious to her state of undress as he prolonged the conversation.

"I hope so. Francesco is taking me to the Calambra in Playa de las Americas. He says they have a great cabaret."

"They do. It's a class act. Most of the performers are international stars." Matt gave a brief nod of approval.

"So he said." Alex wished he would just leave the vegetables and go away. Not only did she want to get back to her rapidly cooling bath, she also wanted to concentrate on the evening ahead, and the sight of Matt standing there dressed in a well-cut blue jacket and navy chinos wasn't helping one little bit.

Matt, however, wasn't going anywhere. It seemed that he had more to say about her evening's date. "You'd do well to be careful around Francesco. He has a bit of a reputation as far as women are concerned."

"Because he likes to flirt and pay extravagant compliments, I suppose. For goodness' sake, Matt, give me some credit! I don't take anything he says seriously; he's too obvious for that. And not that it's any of your business, but if you really must know, I'm going out with him this evening because he's fun and . . . and because he asked me," she added hotly as she remembered Matt's own tentative invitation and how he had never followed it through.

His frown deepened as he pushed himself away from the door. "I'm making it my business to warn you about him because you're working for me, and that makes me feel responsible."

"So you keep a check on Conchita as well, do you, and only let her go on approved dates too?" Alex was furious. "I think you're taking your responsibilities as my boss just a little too seriously, Mr. Anderson. Now, if you don't mind, I would like to go and have my bath before the water gets cold. That is, unless you have any other warnings for me, of course."

He glared back at her for a long moment. Then he shook his head, the vestige of a shamefaced smile curling his lips. "Sorry. I guess I'm just letting my own personal feelings get in the way. Francesco and I have some unfinished business between us, and it sort of colors the way I feel about him."

"Well, don't use it to influence other people!" Alex was not prepared to back down despite her own growing irritation with Francesco's incessant flirtation. "He has always been perfectly nice to me, and if I want to go on seeing him, then I will."

"Okay, okay! Point taken. I won't mention him again, I promise. Now, where do you want me to put these?" He thrust the vegetable box toward her.

Without thinking, Alex put out her hands to take it and then hurriedly snatched them back to rescue the towel as it became untucked and started to slide to the ground. Scarlet to the roots of her hair, she wrapped it more tightly around her in one swift, embarrassed movement.

"I . . . uh . . . I think that I'd better carry these to the kitchen, don't you?" Matt's face, if Alex had been brave enough to look at it, was full of repressed laughter. She wasn't brave enough, though. Instead she just stood against the wall clutching the towel to her as if her life depended on it and waited for him to carry the box past her and dump it on the counter.

He was back in moments. "Have a good time," he said, and then she heard his chuckle of amusement as he walked up the path. "I won't tell anyone if you don't," he called over his shoulder.

She slammed the door hard behind him and leaned against it, letting the cool wood calm her fevered body. How was she ever going to be able to face him again after arguing with him so hotly and then . . . then . . . the towel? She blushed anew as she recalled how it had very nearly been an embarrassment of epic proportions. Nevertheless, as she walked back into the bathroom, the slightest hint of a smile pulling at the corners of her mouth.

Later, however, lying back in the hot scented water, she frowned. Surely Matt had known that she was going out to-night. After all, he had been with her when Francesco tele-phoned, so he must have heard her agree to meet him. In fact, if her memory served her right, Francesco's telephone call was the very thing that had sent Matt hotfooting it out of the house and, until this evening, out of her life yet again.

Although Matt had been genuinely amused by Alex's barely rescued faux pas with the towel, to the extent that he was still smiling as he drove toward Playa de las Americas, he wasn't at all happy. Regardless of his own feelings for Alex, he had good cause to be worried about her relationship with Francesco, and that was why he had offered to deliver the box of vegetables when he saw it on Cristina's kitchen table. He wanted an excuse to call on her, to try to find out where Francesco was taking her, because he knew far too much about Francesco to be optimistic about his intentions. He knew that Francesco was a predator who used his charm and good looks to get what he wanted, and Matt was worried about what he might want from Alex. For a start, attractive as she was, she wasn't his usual type. She was too intelligent, too independent, and, dare he say it, too old. Francesco liked arm candy, the younger the better, because that way he could play the indulgent older man while showing the world that he still had what it took to attract some of the many babes who swarmed across Tenerife every year.

Matt couldn't share his concerns with anyone, however. Cristina and Conchita would just laugh at him and tell him it was sour grapes, because although they knew some of Francesco's faults, they both fell unfailingly for his flattery every time he turned it on them. Nor could he discuss it with Rufino, because he and his friend had made a silent pact to never mention Francesco's name, so there was nobody to talk to and only his own very shaky instincts to guide him.

He sighed as he entered the long road that was the start of the resort. The other thing that was bothering him, although he was trying hard to push it to the very back of his mind, was the sight of Alex wrapped up in a towel. When it had almost slithered to the floor, he had made a joke about it for both their sakes, but while the expression of absolute horror on her face had been very amusing, the incident had added yet another complication to his growing dilemma.

The unsecured towel had confirmed what he already knew, that he found her far too physically attractive for his own good; while her blushing embarrassment made him wonder more and more about what sort of person she really was.

Their chat on her balcony had half persuaded him that there was more to her than he'd suspected at first. She was more serious, less frothy, than her tales about her social life in London had led him to believe. Also, her professionalism suggested long hours of dedication to her work; plus, she had the one thing that was always attractive: an absolute passion for what she was doing, a passion that shone from her very depths, lighting up her face in a way that he recognized. She felt about her work like he felt about the Alcaszar. It wasn't just a job. It was what directed her life.

He pulled over to the side of the road and parked outside an open-air bar immediately opposite the Calambra. Locking his car, he walked purposefully toward a table that gave him a good view of the nightclub opposite. There were bound to be people here he could chat with despite his long absence from the hectic social scene that was Playa de las Americas. And later, if he was still worried, he could move across the road and sit in the Calambra bar, well out of Alex and Francesco's line of vision.

His surveillance planned to his satisfaction, he ordered a light beer. It arrived quickly, and as he took his first sip, he told himself that he was probably worrying needlessly. Now all he had to do was wipe out that image of her barely hidden curves, the one that was imprinted on his brain, and he would be fine; but as his errant body responded once more to the seductive picture that he couldn't eradicate, he groaned. He knew it was impossible.

Chapter Twelve

When Francesco's car horn sounded outside the apartment at eight o'clock, Alex picked up her evening bag, took a final look at herself in the mirror, and then sashayed down the path, fully aware that she looked her very best. This was reflected in Francesco's eyes as he held open the car door.

"Such a beautiful señorita," he murmured, his fingers lingering just a little too long on her back as he helped her into the ridiculously low bucket seat of his sports car.

Alex smiled as she watched him walk around to the driver's door. After their recent argument, to say nothing of the mortifying incident of the towel, she had determined, once and for all, to put any thought of Matt right out of her mind and enjoy herself. To that end, she had treated herself to a single glass of wine while she waited for Francesco to arrive, hoping that it would help her relax.

Although the journey to Playa de las Americas was still pretty hair-raising, Francesco did tone it down slightly, so that when they arrived she was feeling far less stressed than previously. He grinned at her.

"Better, huh?"

"Much better," she agreed, and allowed him to take her arm and escort her into the Calambra nightclub.

Once inside, they were greeted by several of his male friends who were propping up the bar, a few of whom appraised Alex so shamelessly that she began to feel uncomfortable. Francesco, however, apart from raising a hand in greeting, ignored them all and led her to a reserved table for two that had a first-rate view of the stage. As he pulled out her chair, he trailed his fingers along her bare shoulders and whispered something in Spanish into her ear.

Although Alex didn't understand the words, there was no mistaking their intent. Francesco expected a reward for this evening, and she was going to have to use all her powers of persuasion to convince him otherwise. For one brief moment she wondered if Matt was right and she was getting out of her depth. Then she remembered all the times she had had to brush off Rory's friends when they had drunk too much, or when they had chosen to misread her friendliness for something more, and she decided it wasn't a problem. Given that she had only let him kiss her cheek so far, there was no way Francesco could think she was a pushover. Nevertheless, perhaps a gentle reminder would be sensible.

"I'm paying for myself again, Francesco," she warned him.

He rolled his eyes heavenward. "Please, Alexandra, do not mention money in such a romantic setting. You are too independent. Why can you not just accept this as a gift from me?"

She smiled at him, acknowledging his reproof and feeling ungrateful. "You know very well why not, but I won't mention it again this evening, I promise. As long as it can be my treat next time."

"I will look forward to it." The smoldering look he gave her as he replied made her want to laugh. She opened the menu and concentrated on reading it until her amusement was under control. Really, he was so obvious, but she guessed that was why he was popular. He had discovered the knack of making women feel good about themselves.

Once they had ordered their food, Francesco asked the waiter to delay serving it while they enjoyed a drink. He then ordered a very expensive bottle of Champagne and raised his glass.

"To Alexandra! May you have the best time of your life in Tenerife."

She smiled and nodded and sipped her Champagne. It was delicious, but because she had already drunk one glass of wine on an empty stomach, it quickly began to go to her head, so she put it down without finishing it. Soon she was so desperate for food that when the waiter produced a plate of appetizers, she seized the first one almost before he had placed the dish on the table.

Francesco smiled approvingly as he topped up her glass. "I so like a woman who enjoys her food," he said.

"That's because I'm starving, Francesco. Please tell the waiter that we're ready to eat now."

"Patience! Patience!" he admonished. "The evening is young, and you must enjoy your Champagne first."

Ignoring her glass, she sighed and looked longingly at a basket of rolls on a neighboring table. She would have to content herself with eking out the morsels of food in front of her to make them last as long as possible.

By the time the meal was eventually served, her head ached, and she felt sick with hunger. Thankful that she could eat at last, she tucked into her first course: a platter of seafood served with crusty bread. She followed this with a glass of mineral water. It seemed to do the trick, because soon she felt fine, and, eating her main course more slowly, she began to take an interest in what was happening around her. She asked Francesco about the club and the performers, and before long they were comparing their tastes in music and talking about a musical show he had seen when he was last in London. To anyone watching, they gave the impression of being an ordinary couple out on a date, but as the evening wore on, Alex became increasingly uneasy. She had a feeling that Francesco was just biding his time, waiting until the cabaret was over. That there was something else he wanted to say to her. She also wished that he would stop patting her arm or caressing her cheek every time she spoke to him.

She had just finished her dessert when the cabaret started. Francesco immediately moved his chair closer to hers and, draping one arm around her shoulders, lifted her hand and kissed it.

"You are having a good time?" he asked

"Oh, yes. Yes, I am, thank you, Francesco. I'm having a really good time." Alex knew she was talking too much, but she couldn't help herself, because something had definitely changed in his attitude toward her, and he was beginning to make her really nervous. Then the lights dimmed, and she forgot everything for the next hour as she watched the cabaret. It was very slick and very professional, and she clapped hard and often.

It was only when it had finished and the lights came on again that she realized that Francesco had taken advantage of the darkness to shift his chair too close to hers. Suddenly she felt out of control of the situation. Somehow, without her noticing it, he had managed to compromise her. She looked at him. He was asking the waiter for a brandy and, without asking her if she wanted one, was ordering a liqueur for Alex.

Needing time to think, she excused herself, pushed back her chair, and made her way to the ladies' room. Once inside, she leaned for a moment against the cool marble wall before splashing her face with water and rinsing her mouth. Then she scowled at herself in the mirror. She was making a fuss about nothing, letting her imagination run wild, and it was all Matt's fault. If he hadn't warned her off, then she wouldn't feel so jittery. Francesco was just enjoying himself. So what if he had drunk a little too much? She could always take a taxi home. She tidied her hair and reapplied her lipstick. Maybe some fresh air would bring him to his senses. She would ask him if he wanted to dance.

Determined to rescue the evening, she turned on a friendly smile as she walked back to the table, ready to say hello to the two men who had joined him while she'd been away. When they saw her approaching, however, they shook his hand and moved back to the bar.

"Who are they?" she asked curiously, wondering why he hadn't bothered to introduce her to them—or to anyone else at the nightclub, for that matter—even though he seemed to know quite a few of the other customers. It was at odds with his usually impeccable manners.

"Just two work colleagues," he said. "People absolutely not worth talking to."

"Good, because I don't want to talk. I want to dance." Deciding that she was just being petty, Alex resolutely dismissed the two men from her mind as she held out her hand.

Francesco stood up and gave a gallant bow from the waist before taking her outside to the open-air dance floor. Lit with soft lamps that were swinging in the warm breeze, and surrounded by tables and chairs for those who preferred to watch and drink, it was an inviting space for people who liked dancing. And Alex loved to dance. As she stepped onto the floor with Francesco, the tempo changed from lively to smooth. With a smile of pleasure, Francesco swept her into his arms, and for a while she gave herself up to the music. It helped that he was an excellent dancer, and soon they were swinging to some more upbeat music before segueing into Latin American and then back to another waltz.

Eventually, however, Alex's ankle began to ache. She tilted her face back to suggest to Francesco that they sit at one of the tables for a while and perhaps have a soft drink. To her horror, however, he misinterpreted her move as an invitation, and without giving her time to avoid his lips, lowered his mouth to hers.

By the time she fought her way free, she realized, too late, that he had maneuvered her into a secluded corner, away from the rest of the dancers and away from the swinging lanterns.

"What do you think you're doing?" she gasped indignantly, trying to push him away with both hands.

"What you have wanted me to do all evening," he purred, his grip tightening. "Why else would you flirt with me, Alexandra, if you did not want this?"

"I— Francesco, let go of me— You've got this all wrong. I don't want this! I just want to be friends, to have a good time . . . like we've had this evening, so far."

"Good time! You think making silly conversation is a good time?"

"Let go of my arm," Alex said as she struggled in his grip. Why had nobody noticed what was going on? Couldn't somebody see that she was in trouble? She opened her mouth to call for help, but Francesco was faster, stopping her with his own mouth while his fingers pulled at the pins securing her hair so that it began to tumble about her shoulders.

"Let her go, Francesco." A familiar voice cut between them as Alex felt someone take her arm. Panting from her exertions, she shook the hair back from her eyes and found herself looking at Matt. Matt! Why was he here? Thank goodness he was here, but had he seen everything? Had he seen how utterly and totally stupid she had been?

The furious expression that he directed at Francesco as he pulled her away from him told her that he had, as did the tight grip he kept on her arm as he led her away without a backward glance.

Francesco stood looking after them, swaying slightly. He had drunk too much to put up any sort of fight with someone as big as Matt, but not too much to spit Spanish invective at their retreating backs, none of which Alex understood.

"I didn't realize he had drunk so much," Alex gasped as they waited for several cars to pass before they could cross the road. "When we came here last week, he kept mainly to soft drinks, so I assumed he would be sensible this evening as well."

"That was because last week he knew he had to drive you home." Glancing down at her, Matt felt his heart contract. She was pale with shock. He released his grip on her arm and slid his hand down to hers. He needed to get her as far away from Francesco as he could, as quickly as he could. He softened his voice.

"Tonight, as you very nearly learned to your cost, he had no intention of driving you home. He has an apartment a couple of blocks from here, and that's where he assumed you were going to spend the night."

"But . . . how dare he!" Alex stopped dead in her tracks in the middle of the road. "I didn't do anything, I didn't say anything, to make him think that that was okay."

"Except go out with him again." Matt almost lifted her off her feet to stop her from being mown down as a car full of young people, singing at the top of their voices, passed within inches of them.

"That doesn't mean I planned on spending the night with him," she said tightly.

"I know, but Francesco doesn't think like that." Matt's voice became gentler still as they reached his car. He opened the door and waited while she gathered her dress around her legs before helping her up into the passenger seat. Not until she tried to fasten the seat belt did she discover that her hands were shaking. She squeezed her eyes shut so that the tears that were threatening wouldn't fall. What a terrible, terrible evening! She didn't even want to consider what Matt must think of her.

"Here, let me." His voice was full of understanding as he pulled the strap free from her shaking hands and clicked it into place. Then he shut the door and strode around to the driver's side.

He didn't say anything when he climbed in; he merely pulled a clean handkerchief from his pocket and handed it to her. That was enough to unstop the dam of her tears, and for several minutes she sobbed helplessly.

Matt was in torment. He wanted to take her in his arms and smooth back the tangles of her hair, he wanted to kiss away her tears and dry her eyes, but he knew that after what she had just been through with Francesco, the last thing he should do was touch her. He also knew that if he did, his own good intentions might falter, so he sat with fists clenched, silently watching until, with a final hiccup, she stopped crying and gave him a watery smile.

"Don't tell me what you think of me. It can't be worse than what I think of myself." She sniffed.

"Don't be so hard on yourself," he said. "Francesco is trouble, and so are quite a few of his friends. Nothing is out of bounds as far as they are concerned."

Her eyes, ringed now with smears of her mascara, widened in horror.

"You mean he's done something like this before?"

"I've no real proof," he admitted as he turned the key in the ignition and began to ease his car carefully out of its parking space. "But I have good reasons not to trust him. The only problem is, nobody else believes me. Even Cristina and Conchita think I'm paranoid about Francesco because he mostly keeps his baser activities well away from home."

Still the victim of an occasional hiccup, Alex clasped her hands tightly together and gazed straight ahead as Matt drove slowly along the boulevard. All around them vacationers were strolling under the stars or laughing and drinking in sidewalk bars, but she didn't see any of them. All she could think of was what might have happened to her if Matt hadn't been there. Eventually that prompted a new thought.

"Is that why you stopped by this evening?" she asked. "To find out where I was going?"

He nodded, concentrating on the road ahead. "The vegetables were a flimsy excuse, but I needed a reason to call on you to see if I could find out where he was taking you. I didn't think I would get a straight answer from you if I telephoned and asked you directly, not after the way I've treated you whenever I've seen you with him. I'm sorry."

He glanced across at her and smiled apologetically. It was a warm smile that was so full of understanding and sympathy that Alex felt tears threatening again. If only he wouldn't be so nice! Why couldn't he go back to being furious with her, or revert to his normal moodiness? That way she could cope. She screwed his handkerchief up into a tight ball, swallowed hard, and stared out the window.

Matt, after one brief glance, left her to it, and they traveled in silence for the rest of the journey.

Chapter Thirteen

When they pulled up outside her apartment, Alex gave Matt a tremulous smile. She felt more composed now, although from time to time panic still shuddered through her at the thought of what might have happened without his intervention.

He returned her smile. "Give me your key, and I'll unlock the door and switch on the lights."

Obediently she reached for her evening bag and rummaged for her set of keys. They weren't there. She upended the bag onto her lap and desperately sorted through the contents, pushing her purse and lipstick to one side, inspecting a packet of tissues, moving a half-eaten tube of mints. Nothing! Not a single key!

Matt turned on the interior light as she scrabbled on the floor in case the keys had fallen out of her bag when she got into the car. Finally she had to admit defeat. "I can't find them," she said, tears dangerously close to the surface again. "I know I put them in my bag when I set out."

Hearing the wobble in her voice, Matt didn't say anything that would make matters worse. Instead he merely sorted through his own keys. "Here you are. Problem solved. I have a key to each of the apartments on this block just in case there's a maintenance issue that needs sorting."

He stepped from the car, walked around to the passenger door, and helped her down. Then, holding her elbow as if she were an invalid, he shepherded her up the path and into the apartment. Once inside, he checked all the rooms, switching on every light and even opening the wardrobe. Alex watched him anxiously.

"Do you think someone has stolen the keys so they can break in?" she asked.

He shrugged, not wanting to add an extra worry to her evening. "They probably just slipped out of your bag and are on the floor somewhere in the Calambra at this very moment. Don't worry about it. Just make sure that you bolt the door for the rest of the weekend, and if they don't turn up, I'll get the lock changed on Monday."

"I'm so sorry." Alex was doubly embarrassed by the extra trouble that her lost keys would now cause him. "You must wish I'd never come to Tenerife. I just seem to cause one problem after another."

"I wouldn't say that." He paused in the act of checking the balcony and looked across at her. His heart smote him. Her beautiful scarlet dress was limp and creased, and her face was streaked with makeup. She had tucked her hair behind her ears, but the top was still a tangle of pins and clips. Her lips looked bruised and sore, and the expression in her huge green eyes was that of a small animal that just wanted to hide in its burrow until morning.

"Why don't you go and tidy yourself up?" he suggested gently. "I'll finish checking everything out and then make some coffee."

Alex trailed into the bedroom without a word and closed the door behind her. She sank down on the bed and buried her head in her hands. What had she done that had given Francesco such a wrong picture of her? Admittedly she had flirted with him just a little, but that still didn't give him the right to force himself on her. It was barbaric! Particularly as she had made it very clear at the start of their friendship that she was only interested in some lighthearted fun and that he shouldn't expect anything more. Perhaps she had been out of the dating scene for so long that she had forgotten its perils. If that was the case, then she was going to stay out of it for good. What future was there in building a relationship anyway, when even Rory had let her down after years of professing true love and telling her that they would be together forever? No! When she had arrived in Tenerife, she had foolishly thought that she was ready to resume dating, but she had been wrong. She didn't have it in her. So from now on she would be much more circumspect and, for the time being at least, resolutely single.

Matt, busying himself in the kitchen, was worried by the long silence. He didn't relax until he heard the splash of the shower, followed by the noise of drawers and closets opening. Eventually Alex reappeared wearing pajamas and a bathrobe. Her wet hair was twisted into a knot on the top of her head, and her face was scrubbed clean of makeup.

"Better?" he inquired, wishing that he didn't find her just as sexy and attractive in her bulky robe as he had when he'd seen her dancing with Francesco.

"Much better, thank you."

He could see from the unsmiling expression on her face that she had come to terms with what had happened and had made some sort of decision. Whether that involved confronting Francesco or not he had no way of telling, nor did he want to know. It was enough that she now realized who she was dealing with and wouldn't put herself into such a difficult situation again. He handed her a mug of weak, milky coffee, as well as a couple of cookies that he had found in a plastic box.

"Here, this will help you sleep."

She accepted them gratefully and then sat in one of the armchairs and drew her legs up under her. "I feel like an absolute idiot!" she said as she slowly nibbled at the edge of a cookie. "I can't believe I have been so naïve. I guess I've had a more sheltered life than I realized. It just didn't occur to me that someone as outwardly charming as Francesco could be such a louse underneath."

"Not even in London?" he asked, curious despite himself, because he had had her pegged as a woman of the world.

"Not even in London," she admitted. "Although maybe I was just lucky, because I was pretty innocent to the ways of the world when I first arrived. I was brought up in a sleepy seaside town, too far off the beaten path to attract any but the most intrepid tourists, so moving to the city to study was quite a big thing for me. I'm afraid that I wasn't very adventurous either. I know everyone says that student life is one long party, but it's not true. Well, it wasn't for me, anyway. I don't think I did much more than travel between my lodgings, the lecture hall, and the library for the first couple of years. Then, just before I graduated, I met someone, and we started going out. So you see, I didn't even begin to spread my wings until I had a boyfriend, and I suppose that kept me away from the predators."

"Had?"

"Yes. He walked out on me about eighteen months ago when I started talking about boring things like settling down and having babies."

Matt heard the pain of rejection in her voice and winced inwardly. He knew what it felt like. Knew how long it took to get over heartbreak.

"Since then I've more or less given up on socializing. All I've done is concentrate on work. I'm ashamed to say that I exaggerated when I told you and Rufino and Cristina about the high life I led in London. I said it as much to prove to myself that I'm not completely boring as to impress you all. Not that I was lying or anything . . . it's just that it all happened when I was with Rory. He was the party animal, the one who loved going out. Once I was on my own, all that stopped, so when I arrived in Tenerife, I decided it was time to take myself in hand and have a bit of fun.

"Francesco was my first foray back onto the dating scene after longer than I care to remember," she added bitterly. "He was meant to boost my confidence, reintroduce me to the pleasures of casual friendship. It just shows how little I know about anything that I let him take advantage of me like that!"

"Hey, come on!" Matt got up from the sofa, where he had been sitting and sipping his own coffee, and, walking across the room, dropped to his haunches beside her chair. "You shouldn't talk like that. One boyfriend without staying power and one flaky date doesn't make all men bad. It just shows that those particular ones don't know what they're missing."

She turned her head away to hide the quiver in her bottom lip. She was really fed up with herself for being such a watery mess. Besides, it wasn't doing much for her credibility. She was meant to be a professional businesswoman, a top designer, for goodness' sake, and yet here she was turning into a sniveling wreck every time her boss came near her.

Matt put out his hand to turn her face toward him. He wanted her to look at him, wanted her to understand that what had happened this evening wasn't her fault, that Francesco would have found a way to compromise her no matter what she had done, because right at that moment, it suited his purpose.

Then he pulled himself together, dropped his hand, and stood up. *Nice one, Matthew.* How much better would she feel about herself if she knew that everything that had happened this evening was about Francesco getting at him, and that she was just a convenient pawn in their growing feud? He walked across to the kitchen counter and put his mug in the sink. The sooner he was out of here, the better, before he made things worse for Alex by saying too much. He knew from the erratic beating of his heart every time he looked at her that he had already made the situation infinitely worse for himself, but that was something he would just have to deal with.

"I'll leave you to get some sleep," he said, his voice far more abrupt than he intended, because he was suddenly desperate to put some distance between them. This evening had been such a mix of worry, anger, and, every time he looked at Alex, heart-stopping desire, that he needed to get out before his emotional reserves hit rock bottom.

When he reached the door, he looked back. "Don't forget to

bolt this after me," he reminded her, before quietly closing it behind him and disappearing into the darkness outside.

Alex walked slowly to the door and secured it with a bolt and chain before peering through the slats of the blinds in her bedroom. She was just in time to see his car pull away from the curb, and she watched him go in some confusion. His sudden and abrupt departure had startled her. One minute he had been so sympathetic that she had found herself telling him about the breakup of her relationship with Rory, the next he had behaved as if he couldn't wait to put as much distance between them as possible, and had made for the door like a man demented.

She sighed. Although, right at this moment, she was more grateful to him than words could express, she didn't have the energy to dissect his moods. In fact, she didn't have the energy to do anything except crawl into bed and sleep. She just hoped that the events of the evening wouldn't haunt her dreams.

Chapter Fourteen

Alex woke to the sound of a heavy thud outside her bedroom window. It was followed by angry voices, and she hurriedly stumbled out of bed and, for a second time that night, peered through a slat in the blinds.

Two men were walking away from the apartment, and the taller of the two appeared to have the other in a viselike grip. When they reached the pavement, he opened the door of a car that was parked at the side of the road and bundled his victim inside. Alex had a brief view of both men as the interior light came on. One was short and dark and looked vaguely familiar. The other was Matt!

She rubbed her eyes in disbelief and then looked again. There was absolutely no doubt about it. Although she couldn't see his face, the tilt of his head and the breadth of his shoulders as he stood beside the car were so achingly familiar that she felt weak at the knees. What was he doing outside her apartment at four in the morning? She had seen him drive away at least a couple of hours earlier, and yet here he was, apparently acting as her knight in shining armor again and rescuing her from some unknown danger for a second time that night.

As she continued to stare in frozen fascination, he straightened up and indicated that the driver should go. Then he stood back and watched the car as it set off so fast that it left rubber burning on the road.

By the time Alex had pulled herself together sufficiently to unlock the door and call to him, he had gone. She could just see the shadow of his back disappearing down the hill. With freshly shaking hands, she shut the door again and made it secure. Whatever was going on? Had someone tried to break into her apartment, and if so, why was Matt involved? She turned on the bedside light to make it very clear to anyone else who might be lurking outside that she was well and truly awake, and then she crawled into bed and pulled the covers up tight to her chin. Despite the fine night, she felt cold and shivery. She lay sleepless for a long time watching the digital clock flip through its numbers until, at five thirty, she gave up and went into the kitchen to make herself a hot drink. As she did so, she pulled back the curtain and peeped through the slats of the blinds again. To her surprise, Matt's car was parked squarely across the entrance to her apartment.

Without thinking of any possible consequences, she loosened the security chain, unbolted the door, and ran up the path in bare feet. Matt appeared to be asleep, slumped sideways in the driver's seat, but the moment she tapped on the window, he jackknifed upright and glared at her. Then, in one swift movement, he was out of the car and escorting her back down the path to the apartment at such speed that her feet barely touched the ground.

"Inside," he said tightly. "And keep the door bolted."

"Not until you tell me exactly what's going on." Alex's fighting spirit was starting to come back in spades. "Why you're sleeping in your car outside my apartment would be a good start. Despite my stupidity earlier this evening, I'm not a child, Matt, and I want some answers."

He looked down at her, his face slack with fatigue. Then he nodded wearily. "I'll tell you, but we need to go inside. This is not the place to have any sort of discussion, particularly with you dressed like that."

He followed Alex into the apartment, and by the time she had retrieved her robe from the end of her bed, he was sitting on the sofa, his head resting against the cushions. He gave her a tired smile. "I didn't want to involve you because it's not your battle."

"Don't you think that's for me to decide, particularly as, given what has happened to me in the past few hours, I somehow appear to be very much involved?" Alex filled the kettle at the sink as she spoke and then came around the counter to stand in front of him, her hands on her hips.

"Maybe." He squinted up at her. "But it's not pretty."

"Try me." She lowered herself into the seat opposite.

Matt pushed himself forward then and, with his hands resting on his knees, told her the whole story. "I bought the Alcaszar from under the nose of a group of developers who wanted to demolish it and build a huge complex of time-share apartments on the site."

"And I suppose Francesco is part of the group."

"Yes. He's one of the leaders. Initially everything was fine. I made an offer, they counteroffered, and it seemed like a straightforward business negotiation. In fact, I didn't think I had a chance of winning, and I'd almost reconciled myself to giving up my dream, when, right out of the blue, a local businessman approached me and offered to put in some money for a thirty-percent share. It was a fantastic opportunity, and I grabbed it with both hands, because not only did it mean that I could buy the Alcaszar, it meant that Rufino and I would still be the major shareholders."

"Was he one of the men that I met at our first meeting?" Alex clearly remembered the charming Spaniard who had been so apologetic every time the conversation had had to revert to Spanish.

"Yes. And he has no ulterior motive other than wanting to invest some money in the town. Apparently he has fond memories of how the Alcaszar used to be and wants to see it renovated. He thinks it will add something locally that's not available at the moment."

"So once the Alcaszar became yours, the other men got ugly." Alex shook her head in disbelief. "It's like the Mafia."

"You could say that." He gave a tired smile. "Initially they tried to get to me through Rufino. They knew he had doubts about the hotel, so they tried to buy out his share of our partnership with an offer that many a lesser man would have taken. Fortunately Rufino is a true friend. He knows what the

Alcaszar means to me, so he not only turned down the offer, he told me all about it."

"And as soon as they realized that Rufino wouldn't sell, they started playing dirty," Alex guessed.

Matt nodded. "Yes. There have already been a number of incidents at the site, such as broken windows, loosened floorboards, and graffiti, which I've kept to myself. Rufino has already stuck his neck out far enough. He's a family man who has far too much to lose, so my aim has been to keep him as far away from any potential danger as possible. Consequently he knows nothing about what is happening. In fact, we've even fallen out about Francesco, because Rufino stubbornly refuses to believe that anyone in Cristina's family would do anything illegal.

"How bad things are getting was brought home to me shortly after you had your accident at the hotel. At first, when I couldn't find you, I thought that somebody had abducted you to get at me, and I couldn't forgive myself for leaving you alone for so long. Then, when I realized it was just a silly accident that wouldn't have happened if I'd cordoned off the garden properly, I began to doubt myself, but only until I saw the way that Francesco was pursuing you. He was so persistent that I soon became sure that he had some ulterior motive in mind, because you're not his usual type . . . I mean, he usually goes for someone a bit less intelligent, a bit . . . younger." Matt's explanation trailed off into an embarrassed silence as he realized what he had said.

Alex smiled wryly at his discomfiture. "Thanks for the vote of confidence! But, age aside, I still don't understand why Francesco should be interested in me. After all, I'm just the interior designer. None of the history has anything to do with me."

"It's the fact that you are the interior designer that interests him," Matt explained. By now he had pushed his fingers through his hair so many times that it was standing up all over his head. "He's desperate to know what we're doing, what materials we need, and whether we intend to make any structural changes. His group has enormous influence locally, so it wouldn't be too difficult for him to bribe an unscrupulous builder and persuade him to compromise the building, or instead he could make sure that a major supplier strings out delivery times so that we're not ready for Christmas."

"Are you serious?" Alex couldn't believe what she was hearing. She had come across a few shady deals during her working life, but nothing on this scale.

"I'm afraid so, although I'm not talking about everyone in the consortium, of course. It's only Francesco and a couple of his heavies, one of whom tried to break into your apartment this evening in the hope that he would find some drawings lying around."

"So the plan was that he would let himself in while I spent the night with Francesco in his apartment." Alex got up and started pacing the room, suddenly far too angry to sit down.

"Yes, but once I stepped in, Francesco was so frustrated that he either forgot to warn his partner in crime or he threw caution to the wind and told him to go ahead anyway. If that was the case, then I don't know what plan he had for you if you interrupted him, but you can be sure that there was one."

"Which is why you stayed outside in your car all night?"

"Yes. I moved it down the road after I left you because I didn't want to advertise my presence. I wanted to catch him in the act, and I did. As soon as he realized that the door was bolted, he turned his attention to the window. He was so busy trying to force it open that he didn't hear me approach. When I grabbed his throat, he was frightened half to death, and by now he'll have taken the message back to Francesco that I mean business. I drove my car back to the apartment after he left to deter a possible second attempt. I wanted him to know I was still around."

"Wouldn't it have been easier to call the police?"

"And tell them what? That he had the keys to your apartment, keys that he would swear you had given him? Besides, I'm sure Francesco would have told him to make something up if he was caught, something that he would find a way to corroborate."

"And you didn't tell me all this earlier because . . . ?" Alex stopped her pacing and stood in front of him, her chin tilted at the precise angle that always preceded a burst of indignation.

He gave a sudden grin. "Looking at the expression on your face right this minute, I don't honestly know. Maybe I was just a bit influenced by the fact that you were a quivering wreck earlier this evening."

For a moment the chin stayed out; then Alex gave a reluctant laugh. "Touché! Okay, I accept your apology. But you must be able to find a way to stop him."

"I've already tried everything I can think of," Matt told her, rubbing a hand wearily across his face. "I'm beginning to think I'm fighting a losing battle and that whatever I do, he will find a way to get the Alcaszar site."

Alex scowled. "You can't just give up," she told him fiercely. "Surely there must be something we can do."

He gave a half smile when he noticed that she now considered it her battle too, but his reply was firm. "It's not your problem, Alex, and I don't want you compromised again."

She glared at him. "It most certainly is my problem. It's my job on the line too, you know. Besides, I can't forgive Francesco for what he did tonight. If you hadn't turned up and brought me home, I might have been in real trouble by now, to say nothing about the designs being stolen, and how do you think that would have made me feel? As far as I'm concerned, we're in this together."

She was so cross that, without thinking, she leaned forward and gripped his arm, any thought of what skin-to-skin contact might do to her pulse rate far from her mind. "I won't pretend that I'm not frightened, Matt. Francesco has already proved that he can run rings around me, so I probably won't be much help, but I'm not going to let you fight this on your own. Are you really sure that you can't ask Rufino for help as well?"

"Absolutely sure. You've already seen how unscrupulous Francesco can be, so I'm not prepared to risk anything happening to him or to Cristina or the twins."

Alex stared at him, horror-struck. "Surely you can't believe that he'd hurt them, not when he is related to Cristina."

"Probably not, but I'm not going to take the chance. This has to stay between us, Alex, and I don't want you involved any more than you have to be."

He saw the determined glint in her eyes as she opened her mouth to answer him, and he knew what was coming. He had to stop her, for his own peace of mind if nothing else. He took a deep breath as he covered both of her hands with his own, knowing that he was about to say something he would regret in the clear light of day but ready to throw caution to the wind if it would keep her safe.

"Why do you think I followed you tonight, Alex? It wasn't because I knew Francesco would try to steal the designs, because I didn't. I followed you because I was worried about what he might do to *you*."

"And you rescued me, and I'm grateful, but that doesn't give you the right to shut me out of this. I need to help you for myself. Your dream for the Alcaszar is my dream now as well."

Matt sighed. She wasn't listening. He would have to find another way to persuade her without frightening her. Her recent painful experience with Francesco meant that she was still far too raw for anything but the most tentative physical contact, which was absolutely fine by him, because he still hadn't worked out how to deal with his feelings for her, feelings that he knew would overwhelm him if he allowed himself to sit this close for much longer. He had to do something, though. He fixed his eyes on hers as he lifted her hands to his lips.

"Your safety is far more important to me than anything Francesco might do to the hotel. You have to believe me, Alex—it's you I'm worried about."

He had her attention now. Huge green eyes stared into his as she became very still. The momentary silence between them was palpable. Suddenly it was too much for him. He had to break it before things went too far, before there was no going back. He deliberately took the tension out of the situation by somehow dredging up a chuckle of wry amusement.

"And you know how Cristina would react if anything happened to you, so believe me, this is not just for my own peace of mind. I really don't want to have to face the sort of fury she would throw at me as well."

Alex swallowed hard and forced a smile as he withdrew his hands. For one brief, heart-stopping moment, she had believed that he cared for her, that the attraction that sometimes threatened to overwhelm her was a two-way affair. That it was just possible that she had been wrong about him after all, and that there was a space in a corner of his heart for someone other than Adriana. All these thoughts had passed through her head in less time than it took to draw a breath, and then he had mentioned Cristina. Her name had acted like a dash of cold water. Common sense returned. Of course Matt was worried about her. He felt responsible that his problems had led her into a difficult, even dangerous, situation. There was nothing personal about it, and there never would be, so the sooner she just accepted the friendship he was offering, the better.

Besides, hadn't she decided just a few hours ago that she was off all men for the foreseeable future? And all men included Matt! She pushed herself out of her chair, aiming for as much dignity as it was possible to achieve while wearing an oversized bathrobe and pink fuzzy slippers.

"Sorry, Matt, but if anything happens to me, then you are just going to have to deal with Cristina on your own, because I'm in this up to my neck whether you like it or not."

She turned away so that he wouldn't see the tears of disappointment gathering in the corners of her eyes. She was going to forget the brush of his lips across her fingers and make some very strong black coffee to kick their brain cells into action, because they needed to do some hard thinking if they were going to find a way out of this.

Matt leaned back against the sofa cushions again and watched her busy herself at the kitchen counter. He recognized defeat when it stared him in the face. Alex was nothing if not obstinate, as her earlier determination to carry on dating Francesco despite his warnings had proved. If she had decided she was going to be involved, then involved she was.

He gave an inward sigh. Her lack of response to his declaration that he was worried about her, not the hotel, hadn't been exactly overwhelming either. Of course, it might have been different if he hadn't chickened out halfway through and brought Cristina into the conversation, but that was something he would never know. He had been right to take the emotional charge out of the situation, though, because even supposing he could forget the heartbreak that Adriana had left behind and take a chance on love again, now was not the time, not with the problem of Francesco hanging over them.

Anyway, who did he think he was he kidding? Alex hadn't exactly jumped into his arms when he held her hand, had she? It was obvious that a working friendship was all she wanted. Friendship, and a foolproof plan that would stop Francesco in his tracks. It was time to stop thinking about Alex and start talking to her. Maybe they could come up with some sort of strategy between them. First, though, he would have to arrange for the locks to be changed on the apartment, and then he . . .

A few minutes later Alex carried two steaming mugs of coffee across the room to where Matt was sitting. "Here you are," she said, setting his carefully on a low wicker table.

When he didn't reply, she looked at him. He was fast asleep. *So much for my security guard,* she thought wryly as she walked back to the front door and shot the bolt. Then she returned to the lounge area and curled herself into the chair opposite him. As she slowly sipped her scalding coffee, she watched him, noticing how sleep smoothed his face, making him look younger and more vulnerable. She wanted to brush down his hair and move some cushions to make him more comfortable. She didn't do any of those things, though. Instead, she kept watching him and remained deep in thought until the early-morning sun began to filter around the edges of the drapes.

Chapter Fifteen

When Matt woke up, Alex, already dressed in jeans and a T-shirt, was sitting on the balcony enjoying the freshness of the morning and sipping an orange juice. For a long moment he didn't move. From where he was sitting, he could only see part of her profile and the pale nape of her neck, which looked slender and vulnerable under the curls of her ponytail. It was enough, though, to set his stomach clenching with sudden desire. He snapped his eyes shut. When he opened them again, she had left the balcony and was busying herself at the breakfast bar.

"I can only offer toast and fruit," she said.

Damping down his feelings, he uncoiled himself from the sofa with a groan as the effects of a night in the car kicked in. Then he stretched his arms above his head, giving Alex the merest glimpse of a tanned and firm stomach where one of the buttons had come undone on his crumpled shirt. She hurriedly averted her eyes, but not before her breath had caught in her throat. He was beautiful, she decided. It wasn't something you noticed instantly, because his serious expression, often overlaid by a slight frown, got in the way, as did the frequently mussed effect of his thick hair. But when he smiled and stretched his slim, muscled body without a trace of self-consciousness, as he was doing now, he was close to devastating. Slyly watching him from the corner of her eye, she could see exactly why he had met and married someone as stunning as Adriana. With a despondent sigh, she lifted her head and glanced at herself in the large mirror fixed to the wall opposite.

A small heart-shaped face stared back. Her eyes, green with the slightest hint of hazel, were wide-set beneath well-defined, arched brows. She had good teeth in a mouth that was always inclined to smile, full lips, and the sort of pale honey coloring that warmed to gold at the slightest hint of sun. Not so bad, she decided, but a more aquiline nose and smoother hair would definitely improve things. She would also like a swan-like neck, and longer legs would be good too, she told herself gloomily.

Matt's reflection smiled back at her as he pulled out a stool and joined her at the breakfast bar. "Toast and fruit will be fine," he said. "I'm sorry I fell asleep. I guess yesterday was a long day."

As their eyes met, Alex flushed slightly and looked away. She wished she could tame her wandering thoughts. After the experience she had had with Francesco yesterday, she had expected to be off men for a very long time. Matt, however, seemed to be able to breech her defenses without trying—in fact, without being remotely interested in her, she told herself firmly as she pushed the fruit bowl toward him.

He bit into an apple as he watched her rapidly slice some bread for the toast. He could see that she was uncomfortable about something, and he was sure that in the cold light of day, she was newly embarrassed by what had happened the previous evening. Best to meet it head-on, he decided, and he turned the conversation to the problem of Francesco and the consortium.

"We never did get around to discussing tactics," he reminded her.

"I know. I've been thinking it over, and I've come up with a plan of sorts." Alex slotted some bread into the toaster and then took a jar of honey from the cupboard and put it on the breakfast bar. With nothing left to do, she climbed onto a stool beside him and forced herself to look directly into his eyes.

"I want to tell Tom the whole story," she said. "Once he knows the sort of problem we have, I'm sure he'll help."

"What can he do from London?" Matt asked, puzzled by her thinking.

"Well, Francesco won't be looking for anything ordered by another company, will he? He'll just be looking for orders from Miguel & Anderson, so we should be able to outsmart him by sending Tom a list of everything we need and asking him to phone the suppliers direct from London and order under his own name. He can pretend he's developing property on Tenerife, and arrange for everything to be delivered to a storage unit in Playa de las Americas until we're ready for it."

"That's lot to ask of him, considering I've already pinched his best designer for six months." Matt looked doubtful.

Alex shook her head decidedly. "I don't think Tom will see it like that. Although he didn't go into detail when he offered me your contract, I got the distinct impression that he owes you a few favors."

"Maybe." Matt was noncommittal as he considered her suggestion. "I guess it might work, as long as you are sure that Francesco has no idea who you work for in London."

"All he knows from me is that I'm an interior designer. The first tenet of Curzon Design is complete client confidentiality, so every time he asked me about my work and what plans I had for the Alcaszar, I changed the subject."

Matt's sudden grin smoothed the frown of concentration from his face. "No wonder he resorted to trying to kidnap you. He usually chooses girls who are complete airheads, so he doesn't understand the art of subtle interrogation."

Alex gave a peal of laughter. "He doesn't understand subtle, period!"

Before he could stop himself, Matt caught hold of her hand. "I'm glad you can laugh about him now," he said. "Francesco is not worth crying over."

"That's exactly what he said about you when you ignored me at the tapas bar," Alex teased.

Then, as one, they both stopped laughing and just sat and looked at each other, their hands linked. For a long, heart-stopping moment, neither of them spoke, until Matt forced himself to withdraw his hand and start talking about the Alcaszar again. Taking his cue, Alex spread honey onto a piece of toast while she listened to his concerns.

"I guess it might just work, and certainly the suppliers are our weak link. Francesco knows so many of them that he is far more likely to be able to persuade a few of them to use delaying tactics than he is to bribe a builder. I've used the same firm for building refits for years, ever since my first development, in fact. The owner would never do anything to jeopardize the large amount of work that Rufino and I send his way. I just need to warn him not to use any short-term contractors on the Alcaszar. If the work is done by his in-house craftsmen, then we have nothing to worry about."

"So may I contact Tom?"

"Yes, if you really think he'll be happy to do it. Tell him I asked to increase your fee to cover his time and expenses, and say that I'll transfer funds to his account as he needs them."

Alex nodded, but she wasn't really listening, because her thoughts were already concentrated on what lay ahead. When she visited suppliers, she would now have to use her own delaying tactics until Tom could place the order for her. Also, she needed to find a way of working with the builder that would avoid having to give him a copy of all the room plans without appearing to mistrust him. And on top of that, she still had to finish her designs.

"We need to go back to the Alcaszar," she told Matt. "I can't finish the designs for the public areas without some input from you, and we need them finished fast if we are to manage all this by Christmas."

"Come on, then." He pushed his stool back and stood up. "But we'll take the laptop and drawings with us. They'll be safer in the car than in your apartment until I get a new lock fitted."

Leaving the breakfast things littering the kitchen counter, Alex grabbed her bag while Matt disconnected the computer and picked up her folder of drawings. Within minutes they were driving out of town and up into the hills that led to the

Alcaszar. There was so much to consider that a hundred and one things were running through Alex's mind as she watched the scenery fly past. Underpinning them all, however, was one thought, and that was that she had fallen for Matt and there was absolutely nothing she could do about it.

Chapter Sixteen

Alex made straight for the dining area as soon as they arrived at the Alcaszar. Matt, following more slowly, chuckled when he noticed her scarlet sneakers.

"I see you haven't taken the concept of sensible shoes entirely seriously," he teased.

She flashed him a quick smile but didn't answer. Instead, she turned her full attention to the dining room. It was a grand affair with high ceilings and the promise of a bright and airy interior once soft pastels and creams transformed the plum-colored walls and pale marble tiling opened up the floor area. An entire wall of folding glass panels looked out onto a balustraded terrace and what had once been an exotic tropical garden.

"That needs a canopy," she said, waving toward the terrace. "People will want to eat outside during the daytime, but it will be too hot without shading. If you use a canopy instead of umbrellas, then everyone will have an uninterrupted view of the gardens, even those diners who prefer to stay indoors."

"But what about those people who do prefer the sun?" Matt challenged her.

"Not a problem. Just install the canopy in sections, each with a separate operating mechanism. That way you can shade different parts of the terrace according to the weather or your guests' preferences. You could add a transparent sidepiece too, one that could be rolled down on colder days. It would protect diners from the breeze without spoiling the view.

"And what about colors? Have you thought of a color

scheme for the hotel, because if not, you need one fast. It should be simple, and it should be used for everything from notepaper to doormen, from waiters' jackets to table linens. That way the Alcaszar will quickly develop a personality of its own, a welcoming familiarity that guests will recognize when they make a return visit."

Alex's sudden change of focus had Matt's mind spinning. Bricks and mortar he could cope with. Structural repairs and alterations were second nature to him, as were planning applications and architect's drawings. Color schemes, however, were beyond him, unless they were beige, white, or cream, as were the minutiae of table napkins and waiters' jackets. Panic set in as he looked at her. There was no way the hotel was going to be ready by Christmas.

Distracted from her thoughts by his lack of response, Alex swung around and frowned at him. "You haven't given it a moment's consideration, have you?"

"No," he admitted glumly. "I guess I must be a big-picture kind of person or something, because I haven't really given much thought to anything beyond the obvious, such as beds and sofas and stuff."

"What about employees?"

He grinned at her then. "I'm not that hopeless! I've already lined up an agency that specializes in hotel staff. They will find all the employees we need when the time comes."

"Just as well," she said tartly. "Because all your time will be taken up making decisions about the interior."

"I thought that was what I was employing you for."

"Maybe . . . but I can only decide so much. It's your hotel, so you need to have the final say."

He rolled his eyes. "You mean I've got to make decisions about notepaper and what color the napkins are?"

"If you want to put your stamp on it." Alex's response was firm. "I can give you options, make suggestions, but you need to take control of the overall plan, because in a few months' time I'll be back in London and you'll be on your own."

She turned away as the enormity of what she had said hit

her. Time was flying by, and in much less than six months she would be nearly two thousand miles away, back in London in her garden apartment, watering her pots of herbs or cooking meals for one in between work assignments. It didn't matter how often she told herself that Matt was unavailable, or how often she persuaded herself that the sooner they were apart, the sooner she would forget him. Her heart didn't believe her. In fact, right at this moment, it was so sure that she was wrong that it was pounding in her chest at double speed. Momentarily breathless, she stared out into the overgrown garden as she forced her mind back to the plans for the hotel. Were there colors out there that could be brought into the hotel? Could she develop a sort of "outdoors meets indoors" theme?

"How about blue and green on white?" she suggested, once she was sure she could speak without a wobble in her voice. "That way you would bring the colors of nature indoors, and you could choose either blue or green for uniforms, or even use a mix of both if you pick the right shades."

"Isn't white a bit stark?" Matt tried to sound interested as he searched around for an intelligent response. It wasn't easy, though, because he wasn't interested, not right at this minute, not when Alex had just reminded him that she wasn't going to be around for much more than a few months. He should be pleased, of course, because, if things went according to plan, it would mean that his dream for the Alcaszar would be one step nearer to completion. It would also mean that she was safely out of Francesco's reach. That it also meant that she would be out of his reach was something Matt didn't really want to think about. After all, he had already decided that she wasn't for him, hadn't he?

"Not if you choose the right white." Alex brought him back to the here and now as she continued the conversation. "There are well over a hundred whites to choose from; you just need to find the one that best complements the rest of the décor."

"Over a hundred whites! That is not possible!" With a determined effort, Matt stopped thinking about a future without Alex and concentrated on what she had just told him.

She laughed at the bemused expression on his face. "It is, and what's more, you are going to have to look at all of them."

"No way!" He held up a protesting hand. "As of this minute I am putting you in total charge of all decisions on interior décor . . . not just the fixtures and fittings, *everything.* I don't want to look at a single color chart or make a decision about a single drape. It's all down to you, and I promise to abide by whatever you choose."

"You really mean that?" Alex struggled hard to keep the excitement out of her voice, her misery about the short duration of her stay on Tenerife forgotten as she waited with bated breath for his answer.

"Absolutely," he said. Then he saw how her face lit up, and he gave a shout of laughter. "You intended this all along, didn't you? You want to do it all yourself, without any interference."

"Well, it does make it easier. And faster," she added defensively, once she realized that he had found her out. "Because, with Francesco adding complications to the ordering process, anything that will streamline what we're doing can only be helpful."

"You don't need to convince me. I've got more than enough to do without worrying about what color the table linens should be. That's your baby. Now, what else do we need to do today?"

"Well, we still have to look at the rest of the ground floor. It's not all color schemes, you know."

He groaned good-naturedly as she led the way back to the foyer. "Lead on, then. I'm all yours."

I wish, thought Alex as she pivoted on her heels, taking in the vaulted ceiling and the sweeping staircase. Then she put the thought resolutely from her mind and concentrated on the work at hand.

Matt was hooked by her clear-sighted enthusiasm, and for the rest of the morning they each pushed their own worries aside as they debated ideas. Sometimes they argued vehemently, but more frequently they were in accord as they wandered from room to room and back again. Through Alex's eyes Matt began to see space and form instead of peeling paint and garish colors, and he was entranced by the way she opened up the foyer for him by mentally ripping out the dark paneling and visualizing the white paint that would fill the whole area with light. She was open to his ideas too, so when he suggested that they should screen off one or two seating areas to give guests some privacy, she considered it thoughtfully before agreeing with him, only stipulating that planted greenery and flowers should be used rather than solid structures.

"Nothing must be allowed to spoil the wonderful spaciousness," she said. "And if we use planters, they will continue our 'outdoors to indoors' theme, whereas screening would interrupt it."

He nodded thoughtfully. "And we can do the same in each elevator area. That way we can give guests somewhere restful to sit while they wait."

She teased him then, all the earlier strain washed from her face. "You mean guests will actually have to wait for the elevator in this hotel? I thought you were aiming it at the people who are prepared to pay big bucks for a unique experience, and I don't think that covers elevator watching."

He laughed. "You'd be surprised what people will accept on vacation when they're relaxed. The sun and the sea and the friendly atmosphere in Tenerife make most of them forget to be demanding, particularly if they've left behind icy roads and driving rain. All they want is to rest and to be looked after, treated as special, and I will make sure that every one of the Alcaszar's employees is trained to offer just that."

Alex's face took on a dreamy expression. "What I would give for a vacation like that," she murmured. "I wouldn't be greedy. Just a week would do. To have a week away from everything, a week where I didn't have to think, where my every whim was catered to . . . it would be absolute bliss."

"Are your thoughts so bad that you need to escape them?" Matt asked her, curious despite himself now that she was talking personally. "I thought you said you had recovered from the bad time you had in London . . . you know, with your ex-boyfriend."

"Oh, that!" Alex dismissed Rory as if he had never existed. "I didn't mean that. I mean—" She stopped abruptly. What did she mean? That she wanted to stop thinking about Matt and how she felt about him, and how she didn't stand a chance because she wasn't drop-dead gorgeous like Adriana had been. Well, staying in the Alcaszar on some sort of dream vacation wouldn't exactly cure those thoughts, would it? She needed a nice, bracing, walking holiday in Cumbria or Yorkshire when she returned home. Somewhere with sharp winds and steep hills, so that she could wear herself out each day and sleep soundly at night. Not a place where the blue sky was the color of Matt's eyes and the constant sunshine meant that his muscled brown arms and the strong column of his throat were on constant view. She turned away with a shrug and walked across the foyer to the wide doorway.

Matt watched her go with a frown. Something was going on inside her head, and it wasn't good. What was she thinking? He wished he knew, but he also knew that he didn't have the right to ask, not unless he could overcome his commitment phobia, and that wasn't going to happen, not now, with Francesco shadowing them; in fact, probably not ever, thanks to the damage Adriana had left behind. He changed the subject.

"Come on, let's have one more walk-through, and then we'll look at the courtyard and the terraces."

By the time they finally reached the enclosed courtyard, both of them were gripped by excitement, their own frustrations temporarily dismissed as they concentrated once more on the Alcaszar. They knew it was going to work, that the dream that Matt had held for so long was about to be transformed into reality because of Alex's vision.

As they entered, they smiled at each other, enjoying the moment and pushing the thought of the long working days and sleepless nights that lay ahead of them to the back of their minds. Matt leaned against the doorway and watched Alex as she gazed up at the beautiful arches. She was so different from the woman who had sobbed in his car the previous evening. Today she was confident and inspired, as well as quirky and funny. In fact, he couldn't remember when he had last enjoyed himself more. Being with Alex wasn't like work; it was like spending time with a friend, a friend who totally got him and got his dream for the Alcaszar too. If it wasn't for the fact that he was finding it increasingly difficult to keep his emotions under wraps, to say nothing of the internal pyrotechnic display that he had learned to live with whenever she was around, then he would say he was having a perfect day.

Completely unaware of his scrutiny, Alex turned around in a slow circle. "This will be so beautiful," she said. "Once everything is painted white, the detail of the carving above the arches will show up clearly. And that will be the focal point. Everything else must be as simple as Moroccan-style furniture allows. Carved cedarwood tables and chairs, large white canvas cushions, huge earthenware planters full of flowers, glass table lanterns, and, of course, the fountain. It won't need anything else except wine, unobtrusive waiters, and maybe the occasional Spanish guitar!"

Her eyes grew luminous as she saw the picture she had created in her mind's eye. "It will be the most romantic setting in the area," she said. "Everyone will want to come here to celebrate special occasions like wedding anniversaries and engagements."

She turned to him, her face bright with excitement. "That's it! You must advertise it as a romantic venue that specializes in weddings. You only need one happy couple for the word to get around, and before long every bride on the island will want to have her reception at the Alcaszar."

She twirled around again, and then, without thinking about what it might do to her, she seized his arm for the second time that day and pulled him across to the fountain. "Look at it. It will be so beautiful once it has been cleaned, and there is nothing like the sound of running water to add romance to a place."

It took a while for the brooding quality of Matt's silence to penetrate her awareness. When it did, still clutching his arm, she stopped making suggestions and looked up at him. He appeared to be inspecting the fountain, but something about the set of his shoulders and his continuing silence convinced her that he was remembering his own wedding to Adriana. A pink flush heated her cheeks. She had done it again! By talking about brides she had unwittingly conjured up the ghost of his own wedding, and if the torn photo in his trash can was anything to go by, that was something he was trying hard to forget. Not that she considered his technique at all healthy, of course. To remove all memories of his wife and then to destroy her photograph seemed like an insult, but it was his life, and she knew that people coped with grief in different ways, so she was going to stop judging his behavior. Instead, she was going to change the subject.

"Well, I guess we're all done here," she said briskly, pulling her hand away from him. Then, aiming for humor, she added, "Now all I need to do is prepare the visuals, talk to Tom, and start to visit the suppliers, all of which will be an absolute breeze compared to the last twenty-four hours!"

Matt turned to her. His face was stern, almost cold, as he fought and won the internal battle that had made him want to pull Alex to him and hold her tight as soon as he felt the warmth of her fingers against the skin of his arm.

Completely unaware of the effect she was having on him, however, Alex was convinced that she could see the shadow of the memory of Adriana in the dark brooding gray of his eyes. They were amazing eyes, she decided, changing color with his every mood and every memory. She wished she could talk to him without noticing them, without noticing anything about him.

In fact, right at this moment, she suddenly wished she were anywhere but here. It had been a wonderful morning, and for Matt to hand over the whole responsibility of the interior décor to her was fantastic, a designer's dream, and now she had gone and ruined it all by talking about weddings. She wanted out of the Alcaszar and fast. To be in its wonderfully romantic courtyard with a man who, whatever she felt about him, was too full of memories to ever be interested in her, made her feel lonelier than she had ever felt in her life.

"You're not to visit the Alcaszar alone," he said when he finally spoke, his bleak tone matching the expression on his face. "Whenever you need to come here, let me know, and I'll check that there's someone on-site or bring you myself."

Before she could answer, her cell phone rang. It was Cristina asking her how much longer she would be because lunch was almost ready.

She looked at Matt in horror. "I'm supposed to be having lunch with Cristina and Rufino," she hissed, covering the mouthpiece. "How long will it take us to get to them?"

Suddenly Matt's dark expression was washed away as he laughed out loud and seized her phone. "We're at the Alcaszar," he told Cristina. Then he grinned at Alex as a volley of Spanish was aimed at his right ear. "I know, I know," he soothed. "It's all my fault. Something came up that meant we had to drive up here."

Several exchanges later he handed the phone back to Alex. "We're both in trouble, but apparently lunch can wait for an hour or so."

"I completely forgot about it. What will Cristina think of me?" Alex fretted as they returned to the car.

"You'll be forgiven," he said as he opened the passenger door for her. "I'm the one in trouble for bringing you up here on a Sunday and then forgetting about lunch."

"You mean you're invited too?" Alex was even more upset when she realized that both of them had forgotten about the invitation.

"Yes." He slanted a wry smile in her direction. "You'll soon learn that one of Cristina's main aims in life is to feed anyone who looks in need of care and attention."

"And you're suggesting that I fall into that category." Alex tried for indignation but failed miserably.

The dimples playing around her mouth caused a sudden constriction in Matt's throat as he answered her. "You will be once work starts in earnest," he said huskily. "After today, leisure time, food, and sleep will all become distant memories."

When they eventually arrived at Cristina and Rufino's house, Alex's embarrassment was short-lived because nobody seemed to care. They were greeted effusively by a large group of people sitting on the terrace. Conchita was there with her boyfriend, as was Cristina's mother, and Rufino's brother with his wife and children.

Wine had clearly been flowing freely while they waited for Matt and Alex, so the conversation was loud and liberally sprinkled with laughter, while a posse of small children cavorted around the house and garden with very little restraint. When Luis and Nicolas saw Alex, however, they peeled off from the group with squeals of delight and cast themselves at her. Kneeling down, she concentrated on them, trying hard to decipher their chatter and answer accordingly. After a few moments they were joined by their three cousins, all talking at once. Only able to understand one word in four, she looked around for some help with translation and found Matt watching her. Seeing her dilemma, he crossed the room and squatted down beside her. This time his eyes were very blue.

"You seem to have a fan club," he said.

"I . . . yes . . . that is, the twins visited me most days while I was working from home, so we got to know one another pretty well." Alex found herself stumbling over her words as she wished he would look at the children instead of her. He was altogether too close for comfort, particularly after what had happened less than half an hour earlier, which, although it was something that she really didn't want to think about for a single second, she didn't seem able to banish from her mind.

Fortunately, Rufino rescued her with a glass of wine, shooing the children away as he handed it to her. "You have some catching up to do," he said with a smile.

She stood up gratefully. As she did so, she deliberately turned away from Matt to talk to Conchita, but not before their eyes met over the rim of her glass.

For the rest of the afternoon she talked to everyone but Matt. She reminisced, answered questions, and listened to the other guests as if she didn't have a care in the world, but all the time she was only too aware of him standing nearby, chatting to people and laughing with the children. Without appearing to, she watched him out of the corner of her eye. He was so attractive, so charismatic when he was like this. She remembered Cristina telling her that once upon a time he had always been full of fun and laughter, and she knew that for most of the morning she had caught a glimpse of that, had seen the old Matt, the one his friends missed. Even now the warmth remained. As he smiled and nodded, there wasn't a sign of the frowning introspection that she had come to regard as his signature mood. She wanted to join him, walk across and stand beside him and listen to him talk to the group of people surrounding him.

And she would have joined him so that she could hang on to the brief happiness that having him close gave her, if only she could push the memory of what had happened in the hour between leaving the hotel and sitting down to lunch to the back of her mind, but she knew that there wasn't a chance of that. So instead she stayed where she was and pretended that everything was fine and that her pulse rate didn't shoot up to triple speed every time she looked at him.

As they had driven hurriedly away from the Alcaszar, with Cristina's remonstrations still ringing in their ears, Matt had asked her if she would mind very much if they stopped off at his house long enough for him to shower and change.

"I know Cristina and Rufino are resigned to my eccentric dress sense," he said, "but I think even they might complain if I arrive for lunch in the clothes I slept in!"

Alex had slanted a concerned look at him then as she suddenly realized that, thanks to her, he had barely slept the night before. He had misunderstood her expression and shaken his head. "Don't worry. I won't say a thing about last night. Apart from anything else, remember that I don't want Cristina and Rufino involved."

She hadn't bothered to correct him, to explain that it was him she was worried about. Instead, when they arrived at his house, she had followed him in and gone straight to the en suite bathroom she had used when she spent the night there, to tidy herself up. She hoped that jeans and a T-shirt would be acceptable Sunday lunch attire, but knowing she could do nothing about her clothes, she had contented herself with delving into her bag for her makeup and then touching up her lipstick and mascara and shaking out her ponytail so that her hair fell in shiny waves and curls about her shoulders. Once satisfied with the results, she had aimed for the large, airy living room, intending to sit and wait for Matt. Unfortunately, she had opened the wrong door and found herself in his bedroom at the precise moment that he stepped from the shower in the adjoining bathroom.

The rooms were only separated by an open archway, and for one long, heart-stopping moment she had glimpsed the curve of his bare back as he leaned forward to pick up a towel and wrap it around him. As he did so, Alex had backed swiftly out of the room and closed the door silently behind her. It was only when she finally found the living room that she realized she had forgotten to breathe. Dragging in a gasp of air, she had walked across to the window and gazed blindly out at the garden.

By the time Matt had pulled on some jeans and a black T-shirt, she was in control of herself again. Her voice had sounded perfectly normal when she spoke to him, and they had continued to discuss the Alcaszar as they drove back to town. What she could not do, however, was forget her glimpse of his bare shoulders and the curve of his spine as he reached for a towel. So she laughed and chatted to everyone except Matt and pretended that nothing had happened at all.

For his part, Matt was puzzled. What had he done? He

couldn't think of a single thing, but then, who was he to fathom the inner thoughts of a female mind? He had never managed it with Adriana, so why should he expect to understand Alex? After all, she was a lot deeper and more thoughtful than his ex-wife, so she probably had a lot more to hide.

Chapter Seventeen

As Matt had predicted, Alex had very little spare time once the weekend was over.

Lost in the confusion of their own thoughts, neither of them had said much as Matt drove her home late on Sunday afternoon. When they arrived, he had carried the laptop inside and then insisted on checking the apartment again in case unwelcome visitors had let themselves in while it was empty. Once he was sure that everything was safe, he had made for the door with a reminder to bolt it behind him and a promise to send a locksmith first thing in the morning. He had also told Alex to telephone him immediately if anyone appeared to be hanging around.

"Not that I think even Francesco will try that again," he said, stifling a yawn.

Realizing that after nearly thirty-six hours without sleep he was exhausted, Alex had given him a little push. "Go home," she said. "I'll be fine."

"As long as you promise to call if you're worried," he insisted.

"I promise," she replied, and then had watched him walk away from her with a sigh. "Good-bye, Matt," she whispered after his retreating back. "From now on it's work, work, and more work. Maybe that way I'll get you out of my system."

She had gone to bed early, and as she peeled off her T-shirt and jeans and aimed them in the general direction of the laundry basket, she had deliberately made herself think of something else, and by the time she had gotten into bed, she was so worn out by the weekend's happenings that she had slept long and dreamlessly.

The following morning she awoke surprisingly refreshed and very determined to push all thoughts of how she felt about Matt out of her mind. After a shower and breakfast she settled down to decipher her notes from the previous day's visit to the Alcaszar, eager to move her plans on as quickly as she could. She was barely halfway through when the locksmith arrived. He spoke very little English but was cheerful and efficient, so she left him to get on with his work and returned to her computer. It didn't take her long to finish. Then she assembled a priority list, checked her calendar for the first of her appointments with local suppliers, and, everything organized to her satisfaction, pulled the telephone toward her and called Tom Curzon.

"Alex! How are things in sunny Tenerife?" He sounded pleased to hear from her.

"A bit problematic," she said, and then told him the whole story, including her own part in it.

He listened in silence until she had finished, and then asked her if she wanted to return to London. He also asked her how Matt was holding up. She could hear the shock in his voice, the concern that he had unwittingly sent her into a dangerous situation.

"Don't worry about me," she pleaded. "I'm fine, Tom, really I am. I just need your help." And she proceeded to explain her plan.

Tom, to his credit, didn't flinch at her suggestions, and within ten minutes they had covered every contingency, agreeing that she should e-mail contact numbers for warehouse storage as well as her list of suppliers, and that once she started selecting furniture and other items for the hotel, she would telephone him first thing every morning with details of what he needed to order. Then she passed on Matt's message about financing the arrangement. Tom's familiar growl of irritation made her laugh.

"That's a no, then?" she said.

"Well, I certainly need money to buy the stuff, but you can tell him not to insult me by suggesting that I charge him for my services. This will be my payback for his faith in me when my business nearly went bust a few years ago."

"Goodness . . . what happened?" Alex had no idea that Curzon Design had once been in trouble. By the time she had joined the company, it was regarded as one of London's best, and she had considered herself very lucky to be offered a job.

Tom hesitated for a moment, but she sensed he was smiling. "Matt would probably kill me if he knew I was telling you this, so don't mention it to him. The fact is that a few years ago I lost a big order that I'd foolishly counted on. The banks weren't interested, and if Matt hadn't offered to bail me out, I would have gone bankrupt. I paid him back in full within a few years, but it was the faith that he had in me that's kept me in his debt. He really is up there with the good guys, but he never talks about it because he doesn't want anyone to know what a softy he is."

Tell me about it, she thought as she digested what Tom had told her. In her experience, Matt's usual mood was dark and brooding. She hadn't seen many signs of the soft touch that Tom had referred to either, although his willingness to look out for her and his care when she'd hurt her ankle had shown that there was a different side to him. *And that's the side that I've fallen for,* she admitted to herself. Then she took a chance. After all, Tom didn't seem to mind talking about his friend, so why not throw in a couple of questions of her own, questions that had been haunting her ever since she had stayed at Matt's house?

"How did his wife die?" she asked.

There was a long silence, and then she heard Tom exhale loudly. "I didn't know she *was* dead," he said finally. "Is this something that happened recently?"

"No . . . I mean, I don't know." Alex was suddenly confused. "I just . . . I just thought she was dead. Maybe I misunderstood what I was told about her."

"I think you must have." Tom's voice was uncharacteristically grim as he answered her. "Adriana was very much alive and kicking the last I heard, and showing no signs of going away until Matt paid her off with a big divorce settlement."

"Divorce!" Alex's thinking was now so muddled that no other words came to her.

"Yes, divorce. She took him to hell and back. Adriana was bad news from the first day she met him, only Matt couldn't see it. He was besotted, and she took advantage. I don't think she ever really wanted him; she just wanted what he had . . . money and a growing business. Ask anyone who knows him. They'll tell you what she was like."

Except that they won't, thought Alex as she slowly returned the phone to its cradle a few minutes later, all her plans finalized with Tom. *They won't say anything about him at all, but at least I now know why Adriana's name is never mentioned.*

The locksmith interrupted the thoughts that were buzzing around in her brain, and by the time she had dutifully inspected his handiwork, taken possession of two sets of keys, and thanked him as well as she was able in Spanish, it was almost lunchtime. After a moment's thought, she rang Conchita.

"Can I buy you lunch as a thank-you for everything you've done for me?" she asked. Then she added, "Besides, I want to ask a favor."

Half an hour later, sitting at a table near the marina, she smiled at Conchita. "You've no idea how good it feels to be independent again. I was going stir-crazy in that apartment."

Conchita returned her smile. "I believe you. And I like today's new sensible sandals. I also like the sneakers you wore yesterday. Did you buy up the whole shop?"

Alex gave a shamefaced grin. "Only four pairs, if you count the flip-flops. It's my one weakness," she said. "I just like shoes, and most of the pairs I brought with me are accidents waiting to happen on these pavements."

"Only one weakness," Conchita teased. "I thought Francesco Pascual was another one."

Alex felt the blood draining from her face as memories of Saturday night flooded back. "I . . . I'm not seeing Francesco anymore," she said eventually. Then she concentrated on studying the menu, hoping against hope that Conchita wouldn't quiz her.

She was out of luck. When she looked up, the other woman's eyes were wide with curiosity. "Do you mean that you don't want to see him anymore, or do you mean that you've had an argument?"

"Both." Alex sighed. "Look, Conchita, I don't want to talk about it. I thought he was going to be fun, that we would have some fun together, but I was wrong, end of story."

Looking as if she thought it was far from the end of the story, Conchita gave a reluctant nod. "If you say so, but you do know that you've spoiled my day. I was looking forward to envying you, and now you tell me that you've thrown it all away—the flowers, the sports car, the nightclubs, the late-night revelry—and for what? Matt's moods and tempers, I suppose, and the chance to spend all your waking hours working on the Alcaszar!"

"Well, that's what I'm here for," Alex said mildly, relieved that Conchita obviously knew nothing about her problems with Francesco and had only wanted to gossip. "And that's what I want to talk to you about."

For the rest of the meal they discussed the Alcaszar, and Alex explained that she wanted Conchita to work with her. "As well as furniture and fittings, we need to sort out the smaller supplies like glassware and cutlery, bed linens, napkins—the list is endless," she said. "Obviously a specialist company will manage most of that for us, but I need someone to help me coordinate everything, another pair of hands to help me get everything organized, and also someone to keep the momentum going once I return home."

"Matt won't agree." Conchita looked doubtful. "He'll say there's too much day-to-day work and that he can't spare me."

"I've already cleared it with him." Alex smiled at her. "It wouldn't have been fair to ask you without first making sure that it was okay with him and Rufino. If you'd like to do it, then they've agreed to employ a couple of temps to cover your work."

"You mean they've finally agreed that I do the work of two people?" Conchita gave a peal of laughter. "Alex, you're a genius, and of course I would love to work with you. It will be such a change, and—who knows?—it might lead to better things."

"In that case, your first task is to find some temps and get them trained in the basic stuff. I imagine that you'll still have to oversee the office, but we can work around that." Alex beamed at her.

To have Conchita working with her was a real bonus. Matt had said, when she had broached the idea, that she was loyal, discreet, and incorruptible. That meant that if worse came to worst, they could take her into their confidence. In the meantime Alex tactfully conveyed the importance of complete confidentiality, citing possible competitors as a reason for not disclosing any information about the Alcaszar to anyone at all.

Then, as they gleefully decided to share an elaborate and calorific dessert in celebration of their new partnership, she toyed with the idea of asking Conchita about Adriana and Matt's divorce. In the end, however, she couldn't bring herself to do it. If Matt didn't want to talk about it, then she shouldn't pry. It was enough that Tom had told her. Now at least she understood the story behind the shredded photo in the trash can, and it filled her with a sense of relief. Matt might still be brooding about Adriana, but at least he wasn't grieving for her. If his ex-wife was as bad as Tom had suggested, then he was right to throw away every last memory of her. It was a shame he wasn't ready to make new ones, though, she thought miserably, wondering how she had managed to get his story so wrong. Maybe he would, one day, but by the time he did, it would be too late for her.

Lunch over, she said good-bye to a very enthusiastic Conchita and made her way to the car rental company to collect the car she had ordered. From there she drove to the first of the many appointments that filled her calendar for the next few weeks.

Toward the end of the following week, everything was beginning to fall into place. The temps had settled in and, thanks to Conchita's training, were coping pretty well with Miguel & Anderson's day-to-day work. Tom had organized the warehouse storage facility that would hold everything they ordered under his name. Alex and Matt had had several on-site meetings with the builder to discuss paint colors, tiles, and flooring, and now the hotel was a hive of activity with carpenters, painters, plumbers, and electricians swarming all over it as they began the refit. Very little structural alteration was necessary because repairs and the replacement of damaged areas had been completed before Alex arrived. A new and fully equipped kitchen had also been installed. Consequently the workmen were able to start retiling and redecorating almost immediately, and within days the hotel began to look very different as the pale colors and muted shades began to open up the interior.

Alex herself had, by dint of long hours and weekend working, managed to finish all the visuals and to translate them onto her laptop. This traveled everywhere with her, partly for security but mainly so she could refer to it while she was with suppliers or when she was talking to the builder.

Her arrangement with Tom was working well. He was an early riser, so she managed to speak to him before breakfast most mornings, and she had already given him the purchase details for beds and wardrobes.

Conchita, who was reveling in being fully involved in the project, was busy researching which company could offer the best price for supplying the small items necessary to get the hotel up and running. She was also overseeing their new employees with a firm hand.

Matt was impressed. "I didn't think she'd delegate," he told Alex when she dropped into his office late one afternoon to update him on her progress. "I thought she would still want to do everything herself."

"That was the old Conchita." Alex chuckled. "You know, the Conchita who worked for you and Rufino. This is the Conchita who thinks for herself and whose reputation depends on how successful she is."

He gave her a rueful smile. "And we're not going to get her back, are we? After this she'll be looking for something with a bit more of a challenge than our everyday administration, important as that is."

"Think of it as a positive. She'll be your new project manager, someone you and Rufino can rely on."

"Did I just hear someone mention my name?" Rufino came into Matt's office with an inquiring smile. Then, without waiting for an answer, he added, "I've a message for both of you from Cristina."

He laughed when Matt and Alex groaned in unison. "You're right. It is about how hard you are working and how you need to relax. She has invited you both to a beach barbecue on Saturday, and she won't take no for an answer."

Chapter Eighteen

Alex was up early on Saturday. She sat on her balcony enjoying the early-morning sunshine as she thought about the day ahead. While she very definitely needed a break, she wasn't at all sure whether spending a day on the beach with Matt, particularly a Matt dressed in a bathing suit, would provide much relaxation. The only thing to do, she told herself firmly, was to spend as much time as possible chatting with Cristina and playing with the children. That way she could avoid being in close proximity with Matt and enjoy herself at the same time.

Working with him over the past weeks had not been as difficult as she had feared. There was so much to do that there had been little time for their conversations to be anything other than strictly professional, and, because her ankle was better, she now worked mostly in the office, which meant that they were never alone. That, combined with the fact that she had rented her own car and so was much more independent, meant that she had been able to distance herself from him and just get on with her work. Matt, too, seemed to have had the same idea and, apart from once asking her if she had had any more unwanted visitors, had kept their discussions business-like. In fact, until Cristina's invitation, she had been pretty sure that she was recovering from the peculiar effect he had begun to have on her. Now, thinking about the day ahead, she was less confident. Matt in the office with his hair on end and a scowl on his face as he tried to sort out a problem was one thing. Matt wearing next to nothing and laughing, as he always did in Cristina and Rufino's company, was quite another.

"Oh, for goodness' sake, grow up!" she exclaimed out loud, getting up from her chair and going indoors. "First you think you are ready for a fling with someone like Francesco Pascual, and when that goes sour, you start fantasizing about Matt. All that tells you, Alexandra Moyer, is that you aren't ready for anyone at all, and the sooner you get that into your thick head and just concentrate on your work, the better!"

Then she walked to the bedroom and began opening drawers and closets to find what she needed for a day on the beach.

Fifteen minutes later she was driving toward the small cove that Rufino had marked on her tourist map. It was well away from the main beaches and tucked into a steep wall of rock that discouraged all but the most adventurous vacationer. For the first time since she had arrived on Tenerife, Alex felt in a holiday mood. She wound down all four windows and sang along to the music on her iPod as she took the winding road that headed for the hills before it dropped back down toward the sea.

When she arrived, Cristina and Rufino were unloading their car. The twins, still strapped into their car seats, shouted in excitement when they saw her. Cristina ignored them and kissed Alex soundly on both cheeks before standing back to observe her.

"Not bad," she said. "I thought you would be a shadow of your former self, but it looks as if all this work agrees with you."

"It does!" Alex laughed and gave her a hug. "But that doesn't mean that I'm not looking forward to today. I can't believe that I've been on Tenerife for so long without visiting the beach."

Shaking her head in disbelief, Cristina began to load bags into Alex's arms, telling her to follow Rufino. Twenty minutes later they had conveyed everything needed for a beach barbecue down the roughly hewn steps to the cove and had set up camp at the far end within a protective circle of rocks. Although it was still early, the sun was hot, and Alex and Cristina soon stripped down to their bikinis and sat chatting on a rug while Nicolas and Luis explored a nearby rock pool with Rufino.

By the time Alex had answered Cristina's questions about the progress being made at the Alcaszar, and they had discussed Conchita's new role in the company, more people began to join them. Some Alex had already met. Others seemed to be local friends who all arrived bearing food and drink to add to the barbecue. Smiling a greeting, she left Cristina to organize everyone and took over from Rufino at the rock pool so that he could break open the beer and get the barbecue going.

Nicolas and Luis splashed through the pool toward her, their buckets full of seaweed and shells. As she dutifully bent down to inspect their various treasures, Matt arrived.

Pausing at the top of the steps, he shaded his eyes against the sun and scanned the beach. He saw Rufino lighting his barbecue, and, close to him, he could see Cristina in the middle of a group of people, most of whom seemed to be stripping off shorts and T-shirts and spreading towels on the dark sand. In other parts of the cove separate families were setting up camp, and two children were running down to the sea towing a bright pink inflatable raft behind them. Farther away a woman and two small boys crouched over a rock pool.

Even before the woman straightened up, a clutch of tension deep in his stomach told him it was Alex. He gave a rueful sigh as his libido, which he had managed to keep very firmly in check all week, made a break for it the moment he saw her in a bikini. Droplets of water on her arms and legs glistened under the same sun that was setting fire to the streaks of chestnut in her dark hair. She had tidied it into a long, thick plait that hung down her back, and her skin, golden now after weeks of working in the sun, was peachy smooth, and her slender curves were firm and athletic looking. Unable to tear his eyes away, Matt kept watching as she held out her hands and began to walk toward the sea. Nicolas and Luis, abandoning their buckets, ran after her, and soon all three of them were splashing into the shallows hand in hand.

Although he knew they were too far away, Matt still fancied that he could hear their shrieks of laughter as Alex helped the little boys jump over the waves. Against his better judgment, he smiled. They really looked as if they were enjoying themselves.

So what's to stop you from going and joining them? he asked himself. After all, he and Alex had managed perfectly well together ever since he had rescued her from Francesco. Their working relationship was good, better than good, because they were now friends as well as colleagues. The problem was that he wanted something much, much more. Earlier in the week, during yet another sleepless night, he had finally stopped deluding himself and accepted how he really felt about her. What he hadn't decided was what he was going to do about it.

He shook his head in self-disgust. He had to be mad to even consider letting her go back to England without telling her how he felt. He needed to tell her that she had broken down the defenses he had built around his heart; needed to tell her that he was no longer satisfied with his safe, single life; needed to ask her if he stood any sort of chance with her, any chance at all. And what if she turned him down? Well, he was a grown man, wasn't he, so he would have to behave like one. He would just have to add the disappointment to the rest of his broken dreams and start to look for a nice, uncomplicated girl who wouldn't wring his heart ragged or torment his sleep . . . eventually.

With that thought, he hoisted his rucksack onto his shoulder, ready to clamber down the precipitous steps and put his half-formed plan into action. As he did so, he saw Cristina run down the beach with a sun hat in either hand and drop one onto the head of each protesting twin. Laughing, Alex turned them around and pointed them back up the beach, her words enough of a distraction to stop them from trying to remove their hats as they ran back to what had now become quite a large gathering of friends and family. Alex spoke to Cristina for another moment, and then, with a wave, she turned away and waded farther into the sea.

As he watched, she paused and then dived beneath the waves with barely a ripple, the fluid curve of her body indicating someone truly at home in the water. Unable to drag his eyes away, he watched her swim out to where a smooth outcrop of rocks provided an oasis of space away from the crowds. Protected from the wind and the crash of waves that pounded the other side of the bay, they were already dotted with ardent sun-worshippers.

Within a few minutes, Alex had joined them, hauling herself up onto the rocks and then sitting, with her feet dangling, watching the other swimmers before shading her eyes with her hands and looking back up the beach. For one long moment she seemed to be searching the cliffs, so that Matt could almost imagine that she was looking right at him, and true to character, his heart behaved accordingly by performing two huge backflips.

Before he could take the deep, calming breaths that had become part of his daily repertoire when Alex was anywhere around, a scream pierced the distant clamor of laughter and raised voices. Its shrillness, above the ebb and flow of the sea and the crash of the waves against outlying rocks, was so long and terror-stricken that it left a deep silence behind when it ended.

It was a moment before Matt could see the cause of the disturbance, but when he did, his blood ran cold. Far out at the edge of the bay a small child was clinging to the bright pink inflatable raft that Matt had earlier seen being dragged across the sand. At the water's edge the child's mother was running up and down screaming and shouting hysterically while a younger child was sitting on the beach crying. Matt dropped his rucksack and began to strip to his trunks. He was a strong swimmer who, as a teenager looking to earn some easy money sitting in the sun, had trained as a lifeguard, and he knew all about the strong rip currents that pulled hard in a retreating tide. Praying that he hadn't lost his skills, he kicked off his sneakers and jumped down the steps. If someone didn't get to the child soon, it would be too late. The inflatable would either be washed out to sea by the current or dashed against the outcrop of rocks that were tunneling the ocean into a maelstrom of foam in the middle of the bay. Either way, it would be a tragedy.

By the time he reached the sea, several people were holding the mother, her terror reflected in their eyes. Others were shouting and pointing out to sea, not to where the child was still miraculously clinging to the inflatable as it bucked over the waves, but to a shadow in the water that was streaking across the bay. Following the pointing fingers, Matt saw a slim arm rise and dip in and out of the water. Good grief, it was Alex! What did she think she was doing? Couldn't she see how dangerous it was, how quickly the current was taking the child out to sea, and how fierce the fountains of spray were that would dash anyone and anything straight onto the rocks if they got caught in the buffeting waves? Without pausing, he dived in and with powerful strokes began to swim toward the far edge of the bay.

Alex had the advantage. She had noticed the inflatable raft when she'd first clambered up onto the rocks but, because the child was clinging to the far side, had not realized there was anyone on it. When she heard the mother's scream, however, she quickly sensed what was happening and immediately dived back into the water and struck out across the bay. Having spent all of her childhood living beside the sea, she was a strong swimmer, so it wasn't until she pulled away from the protected side of the beach and began to swim across the surging waters of the retreating tide that she realized, with a sinking heart, that the shallow seas around her quiet coastal town hadn't prepared her for this. Lifting her head briefly, she saw the raft tossing and twisting in the current as it was pulled inexorably toward a jagged outcrop of black rock.

Gritting her teeth, she redoubled her efforts. Even so, the

child had slipped from the pink plastic and disappeared by the time she reached it. Taking a deep breath, she dived under the waves. For a moment there was nothing except swirling sand, and then, beneath her, she saw a small, pale shape sinking downward. She surfaced, took another breath, and then dived again. This time she managed to secure a hold, and she pulled the unconscious little boy from what had promised to be a watery grave and swam back up to the surface.

For a moment she trod water while she secured him under one arm, and then she began to tow him back to shore, praying that she hadn't reached him too late. For several moments she thought that she was winning and that they would soon be in relatively calm waters. Then the current caught her, and before she knew what was happening, she was being pulled back toward the rocks as the undertow tried to take them both out to sea.

Kicking out as she had never kicked before, she fought the sea with every ounce of her fast-waning strength, desperately trying to keep the little boy's head above water. Matt surfaced beside her just as she was beginning to despair, his eyes signaling that he would take over. Never had she been so glad to see him. She passed him the child and then trod water with him while he breathed some oxygen into the boy's unresisting mouth before starting back to shore. He swam far faster than Alex could manage. She followed slowly, too exhausted to notice that she was drifting back toward the rocks.

Matt's warning shout brought her to her senses. He had glanced over his shoulder to check that she was safe, and he had seen the danger.

"Alex, look out . . . you're drifting!" His voice was reed-thin as it was blown away by the buffeting wind, but she heard him, and for the second time that afternoon she fought the sea. This time she won, but not before she had grazed her leg on a barnacle-covered outcrop hidden beneath the swelling waves.

By the time she was back in her depth, Matt had already carried the child onto the dry sand and was applying mouth-to-mouth resuscitation. As she waded into the shallows, she saw the little boy twitch and then vomit twice. Then he opened his eyes and began to cry. Matt immediately rolled him into the recovery position and covered him with several towels. As he did so, the sound of an ambulance siren could be heard approaching the cliff top.

Within moments paramedics were running down the beach, and relieved that the child was now in safe hands, Matt looked around for Alex. She was standing ankle deep in the sea, her leg bright with dripping blood. With an exclamation of alarm he ran toward her, grabbing two towels that were lying on the beach as he went. Reaching her, he wrapped them around her shoulders. Then, holding her tightly against him, he walked her slowly out of the sea and onto the warm sand.

"Don't try to sit down," he warned as he felt her legs begin to buckle from exhaustion. "The last thing you want is sand in those cuts."

When she looked up at him, he saw the confusion in her eyes and realized that she didn't know she was injured. The pain would come later when the copious flow of blood had stopped and the skin began to scab. He was fairly sure that she hadn't been thrown onto the rocks, so she had probably scraped it by swimming over a hidden outcrop. Chances were that it wasn't as bad as it looked. Until the medics checked it, though, it was difficult to be sure.

He began to rub her back and shoulders dry with the towels, but as soon as his hands felt the warm curves of her body beneath them, they took on a life of their own. One hand gently moved strands of wet hair away from her face while the other pulled her closer to him, until she was nestled against his chest.

"How many more times do I have to rescue you?" he asked huskily as he tucked a curl behind her ear. "You could have been ripped to shreds on those rocks."

"So could the little boy," she answered, her eyes flashing green through wet eyelashes. "And at least there aren't any sharks out there. They only come out at night!"

He smiled at her then, feeling relief wash over him. If her

sense of humor was still sharp enough for her to joke about her recent run-in with Francesco, then she was unlikely to suffer any serious consequences from her battle with the sea.

As if she could read his mind, she returned his smile and added, "I'll be fine. I'm tougher than I look, you know."

"That's obvious," he said. "Not many people would have had the guts to do what you've just done."

"*You* did, and ended up saving me as well. I'd never have made it back to the beach towing the little boy." Alex pressed closer as she answered him, unconsciously seeking the comfort of his arms around her. She had been badly frightened when the current had begun to take her out to sea, and although she was putting on a brave face, tremors of shock were beginning to shake her body. Matt felt the trembling and pulled her even closer.

"Just hold on," he said. "You'll be okay in a minute. It's only shock setting in." He rested his cheek against her wet hair, too relieved that she was safe to even think about trying to hide his feelings from her any longer.

"I can't bear to think about what might have happened if you hadn't arrived in time." Alex spoke to him through chattering teeth, her face pressed against his shoulder. Concerned, he began to rub her back again, trying to warm her up while at the same time conscious of the softness of her skin against his chest and the firm contours of her body beneath the towel. It was then that she looked up at him, and for one fleeting moment the sounds all around them faded away, and they clung to each other as if they never wanted to let go.

Whatever might have happened next was interrupted by Cristina, who arrived out of breath and carrying an armful of towels. She had watched, terror-stricken, as first Alex and then Matt had swum out to the rocks, but now that they were safely back on dry land and the little boy was being carried to the waiting ambulance, her natural assertiveness reestablished itself, and she took over.

"Whatever were you thinking of?" she shrieked, fright making her angry. "You could both have been killed!" Then she saw the graze that scored Alex's leg from hip to ankle, and her face went pale. She turned away and shouted up the beach in Spanish, calling for a paramedic, and Alex proved to Matt that she was as tough as she had said by gritting her teeth and limping up the beach toward the waiting ambulance.

Chapter Nineteen

Matt went with her, holding her hand as she climbed painfully up the steps; and it was Matt who helped her into the ambulance and who steadied her as it bumped across the rocky cliff path. The little boy traveled with them. He was recovering fast, and he stared at them from the safety of his mother's lap. Although she was pale with shock, she smiled and thanked Alex and Matt repeatedly and tearfully as the ambulance conveyed all of them to the hospital.

When they reached their destination, an overworked nurse whisked the little boy and his mother away, only pausing long enough to wave Alex and Matt toward an empty cubicle. Matt pulled the curtains for privacy and then helped Alex onto the treatment bed and covered her with a thin blanket, keeping it clear of the raw skin on her leg.

"I'd quite like to spend some time with you that doesn't involve trauma or bandages and painkillers," he told her, settling himself into the chair beside her.

She gave him a wobbly smile. "Me too!"

"Maybe we could try it once you've been patched up."

It wasn't the most romantic offer she had ever had, but considering that she was covered in blood and sand, it was probably the best she could hope for. Seeing the funny side of it, she began to laugh. Matt joined in until he heard the edge of hysteria in her voice. In a moment he had gathered her in his arms, and he rocked her like a baby while she cried her eyes out. When she had finished, he wiped her face with a corner of the blanket and continued to hold her close, shaking his head at her embarrassed apology.

"You needed to do that," he said, smoothing the tangle of her hair back from her forehead.

"More shock, I suppose." She sighed, wishing that she didn't have to spend half her time in tears when she was with him.

He nodded as he settled her back against his shoulder, using his long legs to prop himself against the emergency cart. Somewhere between the beach and the ambulance he had managed to pull on a T-shirt, but he was still wearing his damp swimming shorts, and he was barefoot. She pulled the blanket up so that it completely covered her bikini. What a pair they made, and what a disastrous end to what had promised to be a lovely day!

When the doctor arrived, Alex was still leaning back against Matt's shoulder, and she winced when she had to sit up.

"I can see that that hurts a bit," he said as he pulled back the blanket to inspect the mess that was her leg. "How did you do it?"

He continued to probe the several deeper cuts that she had sustained while he listened to her answer. Then he straightened up. "It sounds as if you had a narrow escape, but don't worry, we'll soon have you patched up as good as new."

He glanced across at Matt as he spoke, did a quick double take, and then held out his hand with a warm grin. "Hi, Matt. Why am I not surprised that she's with you? By my reckoning, you're way overdue for another visit to the emergency room. How is that arm I stitched up, by the way? And the leg?" He turned back to Alex with a smile. "This guy is a bit accident-prone. I'd warn you to keep away from him, only by the look of you both, it's a bit too late for that."

Matt grunted. "Very funny, Raphael. And the arm and the leg are fine, thanks. Raphael was in school with me," he said to Alex by way of explanation. "And he always did think himself a bit of a wit."

Raphael winked at her as he left to fetch a nurse.

Alex turned to Matt. "What did he mean about your arm and leg? Did you have an accident or something?"

"More like something," he told her, his voice grim with memory. He paused for a long moment and then seemed to come to a decision. "You've no doubt heard about my ex-wife. What you might not have heard is that she had an excellent throwing arm, and once or twice the end result required stitches."

"I do know about her," Alex offered tentatively, sensing that he needed to talk, that the near drowning had unleashed something in him that had been repressed for far too long. "But not much. In fact, when Cristina mentioned her, I thought she was dead, that she had possibly even committed suicide, and that you were a widower. It was Tom who told me that you were divorced."

He gave a laugh that was completely devoid of any amusement. "Well, I can assure you that suicide is definitely not Adriana's style. She is very much alive, although fortunately no longer on Tenerife. She was the worst mistake I ever made, and I still haven't come to terms with the fact that she's out there, somewhere, living it up on my hard-earned money."

"What happened, unless you don't want to talk about it?"

He shrugged as he gave Alex another humorless smile. "Marriage happened, I guess. She couldn't settle, didn't want to, really. The signs were there before our wedding, but I refused to see them. I was convinced she would change when we started a family. That having children would make her grow up."

He gave a bitter laugh. "I believed her when she told me she loved me and wanted to be a part of my life. It wasn't until after we were married that I learned that lying was second nature to her. That was at the same time that she started throwing things like knives and cast-iron pans if she couldn't have her way. Unfortunately I failed to move out of the way fast enough on a couple of occasions, hence my visits to the emergency room."

Alex wanted him to stop. She wanted to put her hands over her ears so that she wouldn't have to listen to another word, but she didn't say anything. Instead she just sat there, waiting for him to finish.

He leaned forward in his chair and put his head between his hands. "She wasn't interested in the house either, or my work, although she was plenty interested in the money I earned and spent it as fast as she could. And still I kept taking it, partly because I didn't know what else to do and partly because I felt responsible. I'd moved her into a remote house in a mountain village, and at first I thought that was the problem. I tried to solve it by buying her an apartment in Playa so she could spend more time close to the nightlife she loved, but once the novelty had worn off, it didn't make any difference. She continued being irrational—violent one minute, contrite the next—and every day I felt more and more guilty. I lost the ability to think straight, I was so convinced that it was up to me to solve the problem, that I just needed to discover what she really wanted."

Alex continued to listen speechlessly as the torrent of words poured out of him, but when he finally drew breath, she put out her hand and pulled him toward her. "Don't say any more. Please don't say any more," she begged. "I can't bear that you were so unhappy!"

He looked up then and leaned forward, grasping her hands tightly between his own. "I have to, because it's really important that you know what else happened. You see, when she wasn't goading me, she was out with other men. She had a series of affairs that I was too blind to notice, until the end. . . ."

"When she started an affair with Francesco." Suddenly Alex knew what was coming.

He nodded. "Yes, she had an affair with Francesco, but by then I was already filing for divorce."

The final piece of the puzzle slotted into place as Alex listened to him. At last she understood his dislike of Francesco. It also explained why he preferred to fight his own battles over the hotel. Without any real proof against Francesco, his accusations could look like those of an aggrieved husband trying to implicate his ex-wife's lover out of spite.

Before she had a chance to respond, however, Raphael returned with a nurse in tow, and Matt was banished to wait outside the cubicle while they treated Alex's injuries.

Much later, lying back on cushions on Cristina and Rufino's comfortable sofa, with most of her leg protected by a gauze dressing, Alex watched Matt and the twins. All three were engrossed in a conversation that seemed, from the few words she could understand, to be about the day's events.

The sight of Matt and the children sharing one large chair brought a sudden and unexpected lump to her throat. He was so at ease with them, his deep voice gently soothing as he explained everything that had happened. Both little boys had been unusually quiet when Alex and Matt returned from the hospital, and even now, despite Matt's assurances, their large chocolate-kiss eyes were fearful and questioning as they gazed across at her.

"I'm okay," she told them in her halting Spanish. "My leg doesn't hurt very much now. It will soon be better."

"That's what we've been talking about," Matt said. "We've been having quite a discussion about you and how the sea hurt you." His eyes smiled at her over the twins' dark, tangled curls. Alex tried to smile back, but her face refused to cooperate.

She was a little woozy from the painkillers that Raphael had insisted she take, and she decided that it was those, combined with her reaction to the day's events, that was making her so emotionally raw. Why else would the sight of Matt with the children bring her to the brink of tears? Why else would the concern in his bright blue gaze make her feel stiff-faced and inarticulate? She reached out for the glass of water that Cristina had placed next to her and found that her hands were trembling.

Matt noticed. In seconds he had gently tipped Luis and Nicolas off his knee and sent them to the kitchen on a pretext so that he could sit beside Alex on the sofa. "What's the matter? Is the pain worse than you're letting on?"

She shook her head speechlessly. How could she tell him that the sudden emotional pain she was experiencing was infinitely worse than her physical wounds? How could she tell him that everything that he had told her in the hospital had started to crack her thin shell of self-defense, and that the sight of him sitting with Luis and Nicolas had finished the job, so that now she was raw and vulnerable in a way she had never been with Rory?

So this is what it's like to really love someone, she thought wonderingly as she stared up at him, her eyes filling with unbidden tears. Her unprotected heart was beating so erratically that she was finding it difficult to breathe, and the tremble in her fingers was so much worse that she spilled some water. Gently Matt removed the glass and placed it on the small table beside the sofa.

"Ah, don't, Alex," he said, plucking a tissue from the box at her side so that she could mop her eyes. "It's all over now, and everyone is safe. You're just suffering from a natural reaction to what you've been through." He took both her hands and began to chafe some warmth into them.

The twins returned with Cristina in tow at the very moment that he bent toward her to study her face. His own was full of worry and concern. Inches away from him, Alex noticed that there were still grains of sand on his neck and in his hair, and that his blue, blue eyes had dark navy circles around the irises, and that one tooth had a tiny chip in the corner, and that he looked—

"Luis and Nicolas say that you are hungry." Cristina sounded uncharacteristically uncertain as she interrupted them. For once in her life she was thrown. She hadn't expected to find Alex and Matt so engrossed in each other, and she wondered if she was intruding. She remembered that Matt had been unusually solicitous at the beach too, although at the time she had put it down to his lifeguard training. Perhaps Conchita was right about his feelings for Alex after all.

She backed out of the room. "Come, we will make some food. It will take a while," she added as she pulled the protesting twins back into the kitchen and closed the door firmly behind her.

Matt chuckled. "Not exactly subtle but appreciated all the same!"

Alex's eyes widened.

He brought his face closer. "It gives me time to apologize for spouting all that stuff about my ex-wife at you in the hospital. I should have known better. You were still in shock, and it wasn't fair of me to burden you like that."

"You were just reacting too," she told him. "First the rescue, and then the journey to the hospital and seeing your doctor friend—it all triggered old memories. Besides, I'm glad you told me about your wife's affair with Francesco. It explains everything. Do Rufino and Cristina know about it?"

"No. The divorce wasn't about any particular affair, it was about her unreasonable behavior, and so Francesco's name was never mentioned. Besides, they wouldn't believe me even if I told them. They know he's no angel, but they have no idea about the sort of life he leads away from here, the sort of things he's capable of, and because he's related to Cristina, I can't bring myself to fill in the details. They just know that I don't like him."

Alex leaned back and closed her eyes. "It doesn't seem fair that he just gets away with everything. He should be made to pay, somehow."

"He hasn't gotten away with everything." Matt's voice was very soft now, and he was holding her hands again. "He didn't get away with *you.*"

A rogue tear slid down her cheek. It was followed by another, and then several more.

Matt released her hands and stood up, a troubled expression clouding his face. How could he have been so stupid? After everything she had been through today, the last thing she needed was a romantic declaration from him. Good grief, after what he had just told her about Adriana, she wouldn't even take him seriously. Deep down she would suspect that he had been partly to blame, just like most other people did. What was the saying . . . No smoke without a fire? Well, that was what he had been living with for the past three years, a suspicion from everyone, except his closest friends, that if he had treated Adriana differently, his marriage might have worked.

She would just think that he was feeling sorry for himself or, even worse, that he was reacting to all they had been through together and reading more into their intimacy than he was entitled to. And maybe, deep down, she was right. Maybe he had imagined that flare of desire in her sea green eyes, because up until that moment on the beach, she had never given him any real cause to think that she was interested in him other than as a friend. He suddenly realized that he didn't actually have any idea how she felt about him at all, and now was not the time to find out.

"I'll go and see if that food is ready," he said. "You'll feel much better after you've eaten something and had a good night's sleep."

Alex watched him walk across to the kitchen from beneath her eyelashes. He was wearing jeans now, as well as his T-shirt, but his feet were still bare. She took in the breadth of his shoulders as they filled the doorway, and the way his hair curled into the back of his neck, and more tears began to flow. How was she going to bear him being so nice to her all the time? Life had been so much easier when he was moody and short-tempered, because then her desire was at least cooled down by irritation. Now there was nothing to protect her heart, nothing at all.

Chapter Twenty

When Matt arrived at the office on Monday morning, he found Alex already hard at work. From the papers strewn across her desk and the half-drunk cup of coffee beside them, it was clear that she had been there for some time. In two strides he was beside her, his palms flat on her desk, his eyebrows drawn together in a frown.

"I told you to stay at home until you recovered!" he snapped.

Before she could reply, the telephone rang, and one of the temporary assistants put the call through to Matt's office. With a growl of irritation he made for the door and was soon in deep discussion with a client. Alex felt anger and frustration building inside her as she watched him go. With a sigh, she flung down her pen. On Saturday she had finally accepted that she was totally and completely in love with him. With it had come the bitter realization that she had to accept that her feelings for him were one-sided, because he would never be interested in anyone while the memory of his failed marriage haunted him.

On Sunday she had slept for most of the day, and her dreams had been so full of Matt that once she had woken to a wet pillow and found that she had been weeping in her sleep for a future that was never going to happen.

But now it was Monday, and she was feeling sufficiently her old self to be sure that she would be able to hide her feelings from everyone—a belief that she had clung to optimistically until Matt walked through the door. One glance at him had been enough to unleash all her pent-up emotions, and they continued to wash over her as she listened to his voice. It didn't matter that she couldn't see him. It didn't even seem to matter that he had reverted to his arrogant and irascible self. That he was in the same building appeared to be enough to reduce her to a confusion that was an uneven mixture of misery and elation.

She pushed back her chair and stretched, groaning out loud as she straightened her spine. She had been hunched over the desk for several hours, in fact ever since she had woken in the early morning and realized that further sleep was a fantasy and had decided to come into the office to do some work instead. Although her leg was healing well, she now had a sore back, and her shoulder muscles ached from her battle with the sea, none of which she had helped by sitting at her computer for far too long. Not that she had any intention of admitting that to Matt. She slid open her desk drawer, tipped two painkillers out of a bottle, and swallowed them with her rapidly cooling coffee.

He reappeared as she was closing the drawer. He flicked a glance at the bottle, and his lips tightened. "Come on. I'm taking you home."

"You're doing no such thing!" Alex pulled her chair forward again and picked up the phone. "I have far too much to do, and anyway, I'm perfectly fine."

"You're far from fine," he said. He picked up her bag and put an impatient hand on the back of her chair.

Realizing that he wasn't going to back down, she did the only thing she could to stop him. She punched in a number and prayed that someone would answer quickly, because she knew he wouldn't interrupt a business conversation. Luck was with her, and within moments she was talking to the builder. Fortunately he had a lot of questions for her, and by the time she had answered them all, another call had come through for Matt.

With him out of the way once more, she hastily picked up her bag, waved a swift and silent farewell to the two grinning temps, and slipped out of the office. Although she was limping slightly and her shoulders ached, she was perfectly able to drive her car, and as she slid into the driver's seat, she breathed a sigh of relief. *To heck with Matt!* She couldn't afford to take time off, whatever he thought. She had appointments lined up back-to-back, and she also needed to go out to the Alcaszar, so with any luck she would be able to avoid him for the rest of the week. Maybe that way she could forget just how much she wanted him, warts and all.

When Matt discovered that Alex had left the office, he was furious, but as nobody appeared to know where she had gone, he had to content himself with growling at everyone as he tried to bury his feelings in work. It failed, and after an unproductive half hour at the computer, as well as uncharacteristically ignoring all the telephone numbers listed on his desk pad for return calls, he leaned back in his chair and stared out the window. One small white cloud floated high in an otherwise blue sky. It was going to be another hot, windless day, the sort of day that the old Matt might have spent on a boat far out from shore, riding the soft swell of the sea, away from the rest of the world. Instead, here he was trapped in the office with a pile of work, while the one person he wanted to be with had run out on him. Not that he blamed her. His approach this morning hadn't been exactly subtle, but the sight of her slogging away at her desk had roused such conflicting emotions in him that he hadn't been able to help himself.

Part of him had admired her courage. Although the grazes on her leg weren't deep, they were pretty extensive, and now that they were healing, he knew they would be feeling tight and sore. He also knew that her muscles would be reacting to the pounding they had received as she fought the current, something that the bottle of painkillers in her drawer had confirmed. Another part of him, however, had been so frustrated by her headstrong determination to go her own way without a thought for the needs of her body that he had just snapped.

He gave a long sigh. Who was he fooling? If he was going to be honest with himself, then he might as well admit that his biggest problem was that however hard he tried, he couldn't forget the feel of her body against him, the way she had fit so perfectly into his arms, the smooth contours of her cheeks as she had gazed up at him, the damp whorls of her hair as it had curled against her face. He couldn't forget any of it, not the rescue, nor the trip to the hospital in the ambulance, when he had kept his arms close around her shoulders, hugging her as she sat trembling under a thin blanket; and later the journey back to Cristina and Rufino's house, where Alex and Matt were made much of and fed and cared for as if they were invalids.

Nor, now that he was being honest with himself, could he forget Sunday. Cristina had insisted that they both stay over, and although Matt knew that he had no excuse, he'd agreed because he wanted to be where Alex was. It had not been a good idea, however, because the sight of her fast asleep on a padded chaise longue on Sunday afternoon had stripped away the last of his defenses. She looked so small and vulnerable, and with her hair scraped back into a knot and no makeup, she had seemed much younger than her more sophisticated, wakeful self. He had studied her for a long time, drinking in the rich color of her hair, the long sweep of her eyelashes against her cheeks, the smattering of freckles across her nose, knowing as he did so that he was storing up pain for himself in the long, wakeful hours of the night. Then she had opened her eyes and smiled sleepily up at him, and his heart had finally cracked wide open.

If Luis and Nicolas hadn't appeared at that very moment, there was no knowing what might have happened. As it was, they prevented him from doing anything stupid, because he never had another moment alone with her, and by the time Rufino drove her home, dropping Matt off at the apartment above the office on the way, he had begun to come to his senses. He had told himself that it was too soon to feel like this, that he had made that mistake before with Adriana and messed up his life. Besides, Alex wasn't here to stay, so what was the point? In a few months she would return to England, and he would probably never see her again. No, the best thing was to stick to plan B and find a nice, uncompromising girl who wouldn't run his heart ragged. Besides, although he was sure he hadn't imagined the warmth in Alex's eyes, he knew that all she felt for him was gratitude for rescuing her.

He stood up and walked to the window. Bright sunlight lit the pavement outside so that the flowers tumbling from baskets and balconies and decorating doorways looked faded in its yellow glare. He shook himself mentally. *Get on with it. Just concentrate on the Alcaszar, like Alex is doing. Before the weekend, the two of you were getting along just fine. The small matter of a near drowning shouldn't affect that.* And with that thought, he left his office and spent the rest of the day at the Alcaszar, tramping through the rooms to inspect their progress as he tried desperately to immerse himself in his vision of elegant design.

Conchita, who had returned to the office from a meeting with one of their suppliers, watched him go with a frown. She and Cristina had spent a long time gossiping on the telephone the previous evening, wondering how long it would be before Matt and Alex became an item. Now, however, seeing him storm across the street to the parking lot without a word of farewell to anyone in the office, she had second thoughts. Maybe she and Cristina had imagined it, or maybe Alex had refused him. Whatever the problem, it seemed to be sending Matt deeper into the emotional turmoil that had started with Adriana, and Conchita had absolutely no idea what to do about it.

Matt and Alex managed to avoid each other for the rest of what seemed to be an interminable week by dint of staying out of the office. They phoned in for messages, worked from laptops, and spent all their time visiting clients or suppliers. When they had anything to say to each other, they communicated by text or e-mail. Alex tried for a light touch and made hers friendly and cheerful. Matt didn't bother. His were often terse to the point of rudeness, using one word when three would do.

Several times she was on the brink of asking Conchita what on earth was the matter with him, but each time she bit her tongue, because the last thing she wanted was for anyone to think that she was remotely interested. Instead she did everything she could to keep him off her back, including playing by the rules as far as visiting the Alcaszar was concerned, and either telephoning ahead to check that there would be plenty of workmen on-site, or taking Conchita with her.

In fact, as the days passed, Conchita became more and more indispensable, not only as an increasingly proficient colleague, but as a chaperone when Alex actually had to meet up with Matt. Alex convinced herself that it wasn't obvious, because the further the project progressed, the more important Conchita's involvement became, and gradually, much to Alex's relief, her presence at all their meetings became the norm.

Matt preferred it that way too. Conchita's breezy enthusiasm and no-nonsense approach didn't allow time for introspection, and on good days he was able to persuade himself that he was coping. On bad days, like the day he saw Francesco's car driving away from the direction of the Alcaszar, he knew that he wasn't. He knew that Francesco would be holding a grudge, but he hoped he had used every precaution to prevent any more interference with the hotel, which, amazingly, given the various injuries that had befallen Alex and the emotional turmoil that enveloped him, showed every sign of being ready several weeks before its deadline.

Glancing at the car's disappearing taillights through his rearview mirror, he felt a small worm of worry begin to creep up through his stomach. What if Francesco hadn't given up? What if he had another go at Alex? His stomach churned. He shook his head, banishing such unrealistic thoughts. Francesco had every right to be driving toward town, and just because he was on the mountain road, it didn't mean that he had been to the Alcaszar. There could be a hundred and one reasons for his journey, and anyway, whatever else he was, Francesco was not stupid. He knew that Matt was on to him, and he had too much to lose professionally to try anything else. No, Francesco was history, and Matt should just forget about him.

He couldn't, though, and because of that he began to take more notice of the chatter around the office. He wanted to know what Alex did in the little spare time she had, and after several casual questions he discovered that she spent most of it with Conchita, Cristina, and their friends, either sitting around Cristina's kitchen table or enjoying a quiet meal at a local restaurant. He discovered, too, that sometimes she and Conchita would make for the hills on a Sunday afternoon, to walk off the stiffness of a week spent driving or hunched over a desk. They went to the beach as well, but to sunbathe, not to swim, Conchita assured him, seeing the tick of worry in his eyes. She wasn't taken in at all, not by him, nor by Alex. She would have liked to bang their heads together, but instead she played the chaperone, believing what Cristina told her, that when the time came to say good-bye, Matt wouldn't be able to let Alex go.

Alex herself was far more relaxed. Now that the work on the Alcaszar was past the first difficult stages, she actually had a little leisure time, and she found that she really enjoyed spending it with the other women. They were affectionate, cheerful, and uncomplicated, and she very quickly became part of their inner circle. Over a glass of wine they talked about anything and everything under the sun—everything except Matt, that is. They gossiped about everyone else on the island, but there seemed to be an unwritten rule that he was off-limits, and as far as Alex was concerned, that suited her just fine.

A month became two months, then four months, and very soon Alex found that she was counting the days to her return to London, and with each passing day the band of misery around her heart tightened. How was she going to be able to bear to say good-bye, not just to Matt, but also to all the people who had become her friends? It already seemed that she had known them for a lifetime, and somehow their friendship and laughter had helped heal her. She was no longer the troubled woman whose confidence Rory had so nearly destroyed. Instead, she was wiser and more thoughtful, and although she was often consumed with heartache for Matt, and for what might have been in a different place and time, she knew she would survive.

She didn't want to return home, though. She had made too many friends in Tenerife to want to return to the sterile life she had lived since her split with Rory. Maybe she should think about doing something else, move away from London, travel, search out another job with endless sunshine, she mused as she brushed her hair on a Saturday morning close to the end of her stay. Then, with an exclamation of disgust, she threw down her hairbrush, grabbed a thin sweater against a cool wind that was blowing in from the sea, picked up her car keys, and made for the door. She was not going to live a life of maybes. There was only one way to deal with feeling sorry for herself, and that was to do something positive. She would drive up to a tiny craft shop she had discovered in the hills and buy farewell presents for everyone.

When she reached the outskirts of the village, she drove her car onto the grassy shoulder and killed the engine. The view below her was spectacular, and she sat for a long while drinking in the curve of the hills with their outcrops of dark rock interspersed with flowers and clusters of trees. Then she looked up at the houses dotting the hillside on the other side of the road. How fantastic to live somewhere like that and wake up to such a magnificent view every morning. Flinging open the driver's door to take a closer look at her surroundings, she didn't check her mirror and almost flattened a man walking past the car.

"*Lo siento, no quise lastimarse!*" she gasped, horrified at her thoughtlessness.

"I'll live," a familiar voice answered her in English.

It was Matt! She stared up at him, hardly able to believe her eyes. He was wearing frayed cutoffs and a T-shirt, his baseball cap was on back to front, his eyes were hidden by sunglasses, and he was leading a very small white goat on a piece of string.

"You're, ah . . . you're . . . is that a goat?" she managed eventually, struggling to control the laughter that suddenly threatened to overwhelm her.

"Well spotted!" He grinned and pushed his sunglasses up to the top of his head. "Alex, this is Pedro. Pedro, this is Alex."

It was no good. She couldn't control herself. Tears of laughter ran down her cheeks as she gazed at the pair of them. "Do you do this every Saturday?" she finally managed, gasping for breath.

"Only when my garden needs an overhaul," he said gravely. "And don't go thinking I'm exploiting him. I'm about to offer him the finest grazing this side of the island for as long as he wants."

Another burst of laughter overwhelmed her as she looked down at the tiny goat. "Isn't he . . . a bit small?"

"Do you hear that, Pedro?" Matt ignored her and addressed the goat. "She's questioning your credentials. I think it's about time we moved on and found more appreciative company."

He walked past the car with Pedro trotting at his side. Then both of them made a sharp right turn into a gate set in a stone wall opposite the grassy shoulder. As they disappeared from view, he called out to her, "Pedro says to invite you in for coffee, as long as you promise not to laugh at him anymore."

Hurriedly Alex locked the car and chased after them. She was still too overcome with giggles to consider what spending time alone with Matt would do to her peace of mind. When she reached the top of the steps, he and Pedro were both standing beside the front door waiting for her, each wearing an identical expression of patient long-suffering. The sight of them sent her off into fresh paroxysms of laughter, and she didn't stop until Matt had tethered Pedro to a stake in the middle of his very shaggy lawn and ushered her into the kitchen.

"I don't suppose this can remain our secret," he said wryly as he spooned coffee into a percolator.

"Not a chance! It's far too good to keep." She shook her head and hiccupped at the same time.

"I thought not." The coffee percolating, he propped himself against the kitchen counter and looked at her questioningly. "Is there a reason why you're parked on my grass?"

His words splashed over her like cold water. *His* grass? She'd been laughing too much to think about it before, but now the full implication of the situation hit her. Instead of escaping from her thoughts about Matt, she had ended up alone with him, in his house. It was the stuff of her wildest dreams and her darkest nightmares, particularly when he looked so devastating. A twist of desire spiraled through her. How anyone could look that sexy in a pair of frayed cutoffs and a T-shirt was beyond her, especially since the shirt was coming apart on one of its side seams. And the hat! The hat alone spelled fashion disaster, and yet somehow, pushed carelessly backward on his thick, dark blond hair, it just added to his attraction. Staring at him, she suddenly realized what it was. He didn't care. No, that wasn't quite right. He did care, but he wasn't self-conscious. He felt comfortable in his body, so he pulled on whatever clothes suited the occasion without giving them much thought.

For a fleeting moment she thought of Rory, remembering how everything in his wardrobe had to be just right, down to the last tie and cuff link, and how irritated she had felt when he checked himself in every mirror they passed. Matt wasn't like that. Matt . . . She suddenly realized that she was staring at him in silence and that he was still waiting for an answer. She turned away in confusion as a blush washed across her cheeks.

"I didn't know it was your grass," she said. "In fact, I didn't even realize I was near your house, although considering I've been here twice before, I suppose I should have."

He frowned at her changed manner. What was the matter with her? Had he embarrassed her? Against his better judgment as far as his heart was concerned, he wanted to bring back the dimples that had so enchanted him a moment ago.

"Hey, it's not a crime," he said. "The grass is free, and if a friend uses it, then Pedro and I consider it a bonus."

A friend! She felt a dull ache just about where her heart

was. At least he considered her a friend. She supposed she should feel grateful for that, but she didn't, because she didn't want to be his friend. She wanted more. Much, much more, but there was no way that she could tell him that because he wasn't ready to give himself to anyone, least of all her.

Matt watched the shadows play across her face. Something was very wrong. Had something happened to her? Had someone hurt her? That man she had once told him about, the one who had run a mile when she talked about settling down . . . Or was it something else? Was Francesco back on the scene? A surge of molten anger flowed through him at the thought of what the two men had done to her. He started to move toward her, intending to put his arm around her shoulders, until an icy little voice in his head reminded him that she wasn't his to hug. It didn't matter how much he wanted her, he couldn't touch her, not when he was so determined to put his own self-preservation first that he had already locked all the words he wanted to say to her back inside his badly damaged heart.

Over the past weeks he had forced himself to ignore the feeling he sometimes had that their professional friendship was only just managing to stay afloat on a seething maelstrom of emotion; that if he had the courage to tell her how he felt, Alex would respond. *No!* That way led to heartbreak. Besides, he had already thrown away every chance that had presented itself during her time on Tenerife, so it was too late to change his mind now. She was leaving, and he was going to stick to his hard-fought plan. When she returned to London, he was going to say good-bye and forget her. Abruptly he turned away and began to open cupboards and clatter mugs and spoons.

"Why don't you go and join Pedro while I finish the coffee?" he suggested. "He gets a bit lonely out there."

Without looking at him, she went. The little goat came trotting up to her as she walked across the grass to the edge of the garden for a better view. "Whatever am I going to do, Pedro?" she said. "There's no chance of me living with him, but I'm not at all sure that I can live without him either."

The goat shook his head so that the bell around his neck

tinkled forlornly. Then he lost interest and went back to eating the grass.

Alex stared at a view that was blurred by the tears scalding her eyes. Angrily she dashed them away with her hand. As she did so, something white floated at the edge of her vision. She squinted, blocking the sun with her arm. There it was again, a tendril of white drifting upward from a cluster of trees halfway down the hillside. As she looked, it darkened from white to gray, and the tendril became a curl and then lost its shape altogether as the wind caught it and blew it high above the trees. She felt a clutch of fear. It was smoke, and unless she had her geography wrong, it was coming from somewhere very close to the Alcaszar.

"Matt, I think the Alcaszar might be on fire!" She raced across the grass, all her earlier thoughts banished as she made for the kitchen. They collided in the doorway, and Matt put out a steadying hand for the moment that it took for Alex to regain her balance, before running to the edge of the lawn. This time there was no mistaking the fire. The smoke was now billowing across the hillside in dark gray gusts.

"Please tell me it's not the Alcaszar," Alex whispered as Matt pulled his cell phone from his pocket and punched in the emergency number. Two minutes later, coffee forgotten, they were in his car hurtling down the hillside. Neither of them spoke for the entire journey, Matt because he was driving too fast to let his concentration slip for a moment, and Alex because she was terrified. Not of the journey but of what would happen to Matt if his dream went up in smoke. What would it do to him if he lost it?

Chapter Twenty-one

Bу the time they arrived at the hotel, the security gate had been forced open, and a fire engine and two police cars were in the parking area. Apart from the fact that the firemen had broken down the main door, to all other outward appearances the Alcaszar appeared to be untouched. It wasn't enough to stop Matt from leaping from the car and running across to the main doors where a group of firemen was standing, though.

By the time Alex joined them, however, he appeared to be calm. "It's only damaged the courtyard," he told her. "Apparently it started among the wood that was stacked there, probably caused by a careless cigarette butt. They say it's probably been smoldering for hours."

From the tone of his voice Alex knew immediately that he didn't believe it was accidental but that he wasn't prepared to talk to the police about his suspicions. She glanced up at him. His eyes had darkened to the steely gray that she now knew from experience was a sign that he was very angry. She took his hand, curling her fingers into his, trying to bring him back from whatever dark thoughts were consuming him.

"We'd better go and inspect the damage, then." She kept her voice deliberately light as she tugged him forward.

They followed one of the firemen past the reception area to where the heavy double doors to the courtyard stood wide open. The acrid smell of smoke and wet wood didn't fully prepare them for the devastation that met their eyes. Every bit of the beautiful walled courtyard was streaked black, and most of the slim white columns were charred and distorted among a dark mass of sodden wood, exploded paint cans, and burned equipment. Even worse, something very heavy had obviously fallen on the fountain and split it in half.

Alex's eyes filled with tears at the sight of so much damaged beauty. The courtyard was her favorite place in the hotel, and despite the piles of building material and equipment that had filled it for weeks now, the area under the soaring arches had still been an oasis of calm, a respite from the noise of sawing and hammering and the incessant shriek of music from radios kept at full blast all day. She didn't want to believe that someone had deliberately done this, maybe even Francesco himself.

Matt didn't say a word. He just stood there, his hand in hers, his eyes sharp as he surveyed the devastation, but beneath his calm exterior he was seething. How much further was Francesco going to push him? If the hotel had gone up in smoke, the consortium would have been able to buy the site for next to nothing, effectively ending his dream. Thanks to Alex it hadn't happened, but were there going to be other times when he wouldn't be so lucky? He had thought that erecting wire security fencing would be enough to keep the hotel safe when nobody was on the site. Now he knew he would have to employ a security guard as well.

The lead fireman called from the doorway, indicating that his team was ready to leave now that all their safety checks had been completed. Matt loosened his fingers from Alex's hand without a word and walked across to join him. The police had already gone, irritated that they had been called to what they considered to be little more than an out-of-control bonfire.

Alex watched him as he followed the fireman through to the foyer. She knew that he would be asking questions, looking for something that would confirm his suspicions. She sighed. After nearly six months she could read him like a book when it came to work or anything to do with the Alcaszar. If only she could have the same insight into his innermost thoughts.

If only she could have gotten to know the other Matt, the one who employed a goat, the one who had once been a lifeguard, the one who was good with children, but now it was too late. Soon she would be back in London, and the brief glimpses he had given her of that Matt, the one who had been so gentle when she was injured, would be just a fading memory.

Depressed by her thoughts and by the damage to the courtyard, she moved under the covered archway, away from the chaos that was the remains of the builder's equipment and materials. Even now, with the smell of smoke thick in her nostrils and blackened wood all about her, it managed to retain a trace of its grandeur. Disconsolate, she occasionally caressed a warped column or ran a finger along a blackened wall as she wandered aimlessly around the edge of the courtyard. She didn't see Matt return or notice that he was looking anxiously for her. It was only when he shouted that she knew he was there.

"Alex! Alex, get out from under that archway! The firemen say it's unstable. Alex! Oh, my God, it's going to fall! Alex, jump!" His last words were delivered like a pistol shot, and such was their effect on Alex that, unusually, she did as she was told without question.

As she jumped forward into the charred remains at the center of the courtyard, there was a loud rumble behind her. She half turned, and then everything went into slow motion as she saw one of the columns split and stagger sideways, causing the arch to sag and then fall. Chunks of wood and plaster flew past her while shrapnel-like fragments jabbed at her hands and arms. Then another column went, and another, until the whole courtyard was filled with plaster dust. Coughing now, Alex tried to escape the tumbling structure, but there was nowhere to go. In front of her were the piled remnants of the fire, and behind her everything was collapsing. Desperately she tried to clamber over the charred wood, away from the danger surrounding her. As she did so, a large chunk of falling plaster caught the back of her head, and everything went black.

* * *

When she regained consciousness, she was lying on the floor in the reception area with her head propped on a pile of dust sheets. Matt was crouched next to her holding a wet cloth. His face was gray with worry, and his eyes were black circles in the gloom of the shuttered space. Drops of water trickled down her cheeks and clotted her eyelashes. She gazed up at him, full of momentary confusion; then it all came rushing back: the crazy drive down the hillside, the charred wood, the falling columns, and the dust.

She closed her eyes again. Her head ached, and she didn't want to talk to Matt, because she never knew which Matt he would be, and right now the thought of having to work it out was too draining to contemplate.

"Alex! Wake up! Please wake up!" She felt him shake her slightly. Heard a note of panic in his voice that she had never heard before, not even when he had thought his beloved Alcaszar was burning down. Whatever had gone wrong now? Summoning up all her energy, she slatted open her eyes again.

Matt was staring down at her, and this time she noticed that there were gouges of exhaustion in his cheeks, and the grayness of his face was scored with smears of black soot. Questioningly she put up a hand and touched one of them.

He reacted as if a thousand volts had shot through him. Then, with a groan of what sounded like despair, he gathered her into his arms and just held her wordlessly. She could feel his heart beating a tattoo against his chest. Surely it was too fast. Had he hurt himself too?

"What's the matter?" Her voice was muffled by his shirt. "Tell me what's wrong."

He only loosened his hold sufficiently so that he could tip her face up to his. "This is what the matter is," he said, and he kissed her.

It was only a small kiss; gentle because she was hurt, questioning because he still wasn't sure how she felt about him, desperate because he had thought she was dead when she'd disappeared among all the falling masonry and dust, but it was enough. When he drew back, Alex's eyes were wide open.

"You kissed me," she said, running her fingers over his lips and wondering if she was still concussed.

"And unless you object, I'm going to kiss you again," he said, bunching her fingers gently into his so that he could kiss the tips that had been exploring his face.

"Why would I object to something that I've wanted you to do for months?" she murmured, still half convinced that her hearing had been affected by her bang on the head.

He drew back then and looked at her long and hard. She responded by licking her lips in unconscious invitation. It was his final undoing, and for a long time after that the silence of the Alcaszar was unbroken except for the smallest of sighs as they explored each other's mouths with a growing passion that was totally at odds with their grimy appearance and the injuries they had both sustained. Even the arrival of the ambulance crew failed to douse their feelings, and although Matt insisted that she lie on the stretcher, he sat beside her and held her close all the way to the hospital.

"I've been such a fool, Alex. It took seeing you nearly get killed yet again for me to admit to myself that I can't contemplate living without you. Can you ever forgive me for being so stupid, for not admitting to myself, or to you, that I was falling in love with you? I have wasted so much time, and all because I wasn't prepared to take a second chance on love!"

She shook her head, her green eyes clouding slightly as she acknowledged why he had struggled with what his heart had been telling him for so long. How Adriana had very nearly destroyed all that was best in him.

"Don't say another word. It's over, Matt! We have beaten Adriana and Francesco. Now it's just you and me."

He stared down at her, and the hand that had been smoothing back her hair stilled as her words made him realize that she understood why he had behaved as he did. As their eyes met and he saw her love for him reflected in their green depths, the sharp loneliness that had filled his days and nights for the past three years vanished as if it had never been. He would never have to explain himself to Alex or worry about her reactions.

She loved him for who he was. Not for his money or his property, not for what she could get out of him. She loved *him*. He had been a fool to think that life was better lived without love, and he couldn't blame Adriana for that. She might have been the catalyst, but he couldn't blame anyone other than himself for his cowardly decision to play it safe for the rest of his life.

He hugged Alex to him as the ambulance pulled into the emergency bay at the hospital and the paramedic busied himself getting ready to off-load his uncooperative passengers. "Promise me one thing, though. Promise me that you'll stop having accidents for a while, because my blood pressure won't stand it, and besides, an ambulance ride is not my idea of a romantic journey."

"I promise," she said, and she put her arms around his neck and kissed him as he lifted her off the stretcher and carried her into the emergency department and to the smiling ministrations of Doctor Raphael.

Epilogue

Matt slipped his arm around Alex's waist and, pulling her toward him, brushed the suggestion of a kiss onto the vulnerable spot where her neck curved into her shoulder. He chuckled when he heard her sharp intake of breath.

"Time to leave our guests," he murmured.

"We can't go yet," she protested, trying to ignore the warmth that was curling up through her body as his fingers settled on the underside of her breast. "Some of them have traveled halfway across the world to be here."

"And they'll still be here tomorrow and next week, whereas we only have one wedding night. Besides, I'm fed up with sharing you. Do you realize that we haven't had a moment alone together since your family arrived two weeks ago?"

She looked at him then, and despite her teasing smile, he saw that her eyes mirrored the frustrated desire that was beginning to threaten his sanity. "Poor Matt! I told you that we should just live together. That way you could have avoided all this."

"No chance!" He pulled her close, and together they watched their guests talking and laughing as they sipped wine and piled plates with food. Soft music wafted from the ballroom, where the more energetic were dancing, while small children chased one another or hid under the tables.

"It works, doesn't it? It really works." Alex squeezed his hand. "The Alcaszar has come to life today. It's going to be such a success."

He groaned. "And I thought *I* was obsessive! You're not supposed to think about work on your wedding day."

"The Alcaszar is not work," she protested. "The Alcaszar is us, Matt! It's a symbol of who we are."

He smiled at the passion in her voice. It was one of the things he loved most about her, and he knew she was right. They had met each other because of the Alcaszar. It had bound them together as they fought deadlines and problems. It had broken down their emotional reserves as they shared ideas and dreams. And finally, the destruction of the best part of its beauty had brought them together. Now, with the courtyard rebuilt and the refit completed two weeks early, they could at last concentrate on their new life together.

Although, once they had admitted their feelings for each other, there had never been any thought of Alex returning to London except for one short trip to wind up her contract with a very understanding Tom and to sublet her flat, the past few months had still been a time of unbearable frustration. It had been a horrific time of sleep-deprived nights and of days with barely time for meals. Both of them had suffered as their hectic work schedule bit into the hours they tried to carve out for each other. Then, with the hotel complete except for the finishing touches, they had begun to look forward to some downtime before their wedding, forgetting that both sets of parents and all their friends would have very different ideas.

With the arrival of Alex's entire family two weeks earlier, they had been caught up in a whirl of socializing as everyone got to know one another. Also, under her mother's supervision, Alex had meekly succumbed to dress fittings and a facial and manicure, as well as a visit to the hairdresser. Now Matt had had enough. He wanted her to himself.

Without a word he pulled her to him and kissed her hard, his lips saying everything that his heart was feeling. Then he took her hand and led her toward the courtyard.

It was empty now except for moths that spiraled in a crazy dance around the soft light of the wall sconces. Matt and Alex were entranced at the unexpected magic of it all. Until now

they had not had time to savor it at night, and they were mesmerized by the soaring shadows that arched the courtyard and
the graceful arcs of illuminated spray in the resurrected white
marble fountain. Over it all wafted the sweet scent of jasmine.

Although the slim white columns that supported the arches
were still twined with bougainvillea, and the large terra-cotta
urns still overflowed with trailing white geraniums, it was very
different from earlier in the day when their guests had wit-
nessed their simple wedding ceremony. This had taken place
under a huge white canopy that had shaded the open courtyard
from a sun that had risen early and a blue sky that had promised to stay cloudless until evening. Now, however, the canopy
was gone, and the rows of chairs had been removed, and the
courtyard had regained its serenity.

"It's so beautiful," Alex whispered, her eyes shining. "It's
everything we dreamed of, Matt. And you have to admit, it's a
wonderful wedding venue."

He laughed then and folded her into his arms. "Okay, you
win, Mrs. Anderson! Conchita will advertise the Alcaszar as a
bridal venue just as soon as we've had our honeymoon."

He kissed her again, a long and lingering kiss. Then he led
her to a small doorway set in the outer wall, unlocked it, and
pulled her through.

Like naughty children they tiptoed across the driveway
hand in hand, staying in the shadows until they reached Matt's
car. Only the smiling security guard who raised the exit bar-
rier saw them go.

Within minutes they were speeding up the mountain road
to Matt's house. *Our house now,* thought Alex as he pulled up
outside the sturdy gateway.

"Stay there until I open the garage," he said. "You're not
dressed for dusty roadsides."

But Alex was already out of the car, her elegant wedding
sandals swinging from her fingers and her silk dress bunched
carelessly in her hand. Moonlight silvered the curve of her
cheek and dusted the curling tendrils of her hair. Matt's breath
caught in his throat. She had never looked so beautiful. He

opened his arms, and she flew into them, murmuring promises into his ear as he carried her over the threshold of the house that had once seemed so joyless and now was so full of life.

If anyone heard or saw anything else through the long night and the lazy days that followed, it was only a little white goat, and he kept his own counsel!